ROSE OF SKIBBEREEN

BOOK 6

By John McDonnell

Discover other titles at John McDonnell's Amazon page:
amazon.com/author/johnmcdonnell

FOREWORD

This is Book Six in the *Rose Of Skibbereen* series, a group of fictional stories about Rose Sullivan Morley from Skibbereen, in County Cork, Ireland.

In Book Five I gave a summary of what's happened so far in the story, but this time I am just going to start in with the next installment. There are around 250,000 words of this story already published in the five books before this one, and it's hard to condense all that into a few hundred words of a synopsis.

A lot has happened in this story, and if you're not familiar with it, I recommend buying some of the earlier *Rose Of Skibbereen* books just to help you get up to speed. There are all sorts of echoes from one book to the next, and the story is more fun to read if you know all the characters and the twists and turns of their lives.

There's one more book in the series after this one. It's called *Mary's Secret*, and it's about Mary Driscoll, a beloved character from Book One. I recommend it if you'd like to revisit the world of the first *Rose Of Skibbereen* book.

But this is Book Six, and the main character in this book is Rosalie Morley. She is the great-great granddaughter of Rose Sullivan Morley, the original Rose of Skibbereen. The series started in the 1880s, and with Book Six I've brought it up to the present time. Rosalie is a special character, with a unique perspective on the world. I hope you enjoy experiencing the story from her point of view.

She certainly has quite a story to tell!

CHAPTER ONE

My name is Rosalie Morley, and I had a boyfriend who thought I was a witch. I guess that's not the way most people would introduce themselves, but I've never been like most people.

I've always been different, seen things differently than other people, and had different thoughts and dreams. I don't know if that makes me a witch, but it means I'm not like everybody else.

I think I'm somewhere on the Autism spectrum, but who knows where? Who knows what little spot I occupy, all to myself? Because I'm not like someone with Autism, either. You can't put me in that box. I went through some testing once, when I was younger, but the doctors couldn't give my parents a clear-cut diagnosis. I'm high functioning, not one of those people who can't speak or look you in the eye. Well, actually, I don't really enjoy looking at people's faces, although I can do it if I have to. But, anyway, I can function in society, and get along pretty well. I am very good at some things, like word games and music and computers, plus putting colors and patterns together. And identifying birds, I'm real good at that. I'm not good at other things, like understanding poetry, or emotions, or people, for that matter. People make me scratch my head sometimes, and there have been long stretches in my life where I've just tried to avoid them.

I live in an apartment in New Hope, Pennsylvania, close to the Delaware River. It's a quaint little town with lots of history, and a lot of artists and musicians and writers live here. I grew up here during my high school years, and my parents, Pete and Betty, still live nearby.

I should tell you about them. Pete, my dad, is part of a crazy Irish American family, and his mother, Rosie, was one of the craziest. She had a great singing voice and lived in London during the Swinging Sixties, then moved back to Philadelphia, and eventually she opened a bar and restaurant in New Hope, which is how we all ended up here. My mother Betty is African American, and she is a lot calmer, more sedate, even classier than Pete. She grew up in Philadelphia and her family were all God-fearing people, the kind who got dressed up to go to church on Sunday and stayed dressed up the rest of the day. My brother Martin got more of the genes from that side of the family. He's got more class, more sophistication, than I'll ever have.

I'm like my father Pete. I'm stubborn like him, that's one thing. If he makes his mind up to do something you just get out of his way, because you'll never sway him. I'm like that. Stubborn, to the point of stupidity sometimes.

In one big way I'm not like Pete at all. I see visions and hear voices, which never happens to Pete. Or, at least he doesn't admit it if it does happen to him.

Visions and voices, that's the kind of stuff that happened to my grandmother Rosie. She told me all about the music and voices she'd hear at odd times. When I was a little girl and I told her it happened to me, she said, "It's something the women in our family have. We're descended from Irish witches, at least that's what I think. It's a blessing and a curse."

So, you see, maybe I am a witch. I mean, it's in my family, right? I never took it seriously, because just because you don't understand something doesn't mean you have to get all spooky about it. I always thought my visions and voices were probably

3

something going on in my brain -- maybe like epilepsy or something like that -- and there was no supernatural reason for them. That's what I thought for most of my life.

Now, I'm not so sure. There are times when the visions and the voices can seem so real, almost more real than anything else.

Like the vision I have in my head of when Rosie died. That's one that I can revisit anytime, and it's exactly like the night it happened.

It was 12:02 AM on January 1, 2000. I like to remember dates, because knowing a date lets you fix events in time, and I am fascinated by time. The place was my grandmother Rosie's bar-restaurant in New Hope called Skibbereen.

Rosie had built this bar and restaurant into a local institution, a place where you could get good food, hang out at the carved oak bar, and listen to some great music. Rosie had a beautiful voice -- she'd been a Big Band singer as a teenager in the 1940s, and it was a treat to hear her sit in with whatever band was playing and launch into some hit from that era.

She had a gift for music, and she had golden ears. She had been in the record collecting business and she knew everything there was to know about doo wop, she could tell you the names of every member of these obscure groups from the 1950s that had one hit and then disappeared. She was amazing that way. I think I get my love of detail from her.

I probably got my musical talent from her also. When I was really little, the story goes, Rosie heard me picking out one of her songs on the old piano in my parents' house, and she told everybody I had a gift. She paid for lessons but I didn't like the piano teacher and I wasn't interested in learning notes and doing scales, so that didn't last long. I taught myself to play by ear, and by the time I was 12 years old I could play hundreds of songs, exactly the way I heard them on the radio. I can't explain it; I just figure a song out, is all.

When I got older I played in different bands, just fooling around, although I never stuck with any of them. Like I said, getting along with people has been my biggest challenge, and it was always easier for me to just quit than to keep trying to deal with all the personalities in a band.

But Rosie thought it would be good for me to play with other people, so she got me into a little jazz trio that played sometimes in her bar. I enjoyed it, and I basically just kept my head down and played, getting lost in the patterns of the harmonies.

So I was there on the New Year's Eve of the end of the millennium, 2000, playing with the group, when it happened.

People were all talking about the great Y2K crisis, when the world was supposed to come to an end because all the computers were going to crash. You remember that? You couldn't get away from it in the years leading up to 2000, even though my dad Pete, who is a computer guy, said it was all a load of horse manure, that the powers that be wouldn't let the computers crash like that.

Anyway, this was a special New Year's, and everybody was making jokes about the end of the world happening at the stroke of midnight, all that stuff.

Rosie was in a strange mood that night, I remember, and although I couldn't describe it at the time I guess it was kind of distracted, preoccupied. One time she was coming downstairs from her apartment above the restaurant, and she grabbed me by the arm

5

and pushed me into a corner by the kitchen. She got right in front of me and cupped my chin in her hand so I had to look at her face.

"What's the matter, Gran?" I said.

"I saw her again," she said. "The old Irish woman with the white hair, and the long black dress. She was saying something again, but she doesn't talk in English. I couldn't understand her."

Rosie had told me this before, this vision she had of an old Irishwoman. It wasn't her grandmother, whom she'd known as a young woman. Still, she thought it was somebody related to her, like a great grandmother. She'd seen her a few times, and it always spooked her.

"You're just being emotional," I said. "It's all this Y2K talk about the end of the world coming."

"Yeah, maybe," Rosie said, looking away, toward the street. "I'm sure it's nothing. You should get back to your piano, honey. It's almost midnight, and those people out there need some music."

She smiled and walked away, and those were the last words she spoke to me.

When the clock struck midnight I was in the middle of playing a jazzy version of "Auld Lang Syne" and the crowd was singing and toasting and kissing each other, and I wasn't even thinking about Rosie. Some of the party spilled out into the street, with people trying to make as much noise as possible to welcome the new millennium. It was hard in the middle of all that noise and pandemonium to make out the screaming, but I noticed people bursting through the front door and yelling, and they weren't celebrating, they looked stunned.

I made my way over to them and that's when I heard a woman screaming, "Call the police! She's in the street! The car just ran her down. He must have been drunk!"

I pushed my way out the front door and that's when I saw it: there was a body in the street almost right in front of the restaurant, and it was my grandmother Rosie.

CHAPTER TWO

I don't know if you have pictures in your head that never go away, like a photograph in an album that you can look at anytime you want, but I do. I have pictures that never change; they're always there in my mind exactly the same as when I first saw them. That's what that picture is like in my mind, of my grandmother lying face down in the street. It had been snowing for a few hours, and there was a coating of white everywhere, and the snow was still falling. What is so clear is that already, even though the accident had only happened a minute or two before, there was already a dusting of snow on her body, white powder that got in her brown hair and fell in the pool of blood on the street. She was wearing a black overcoat over a green dress, and she had silver dangling earrings on. That's the thing that is so clear, those earrings. I know they were a gift from her fiancé Jack Caldwell; maybe that's why they stick out in my mind. She was so still, so completely still, as if she was sleeping, but the deepest sleep imaginable. I don't remember any noise, although I'm sure there was lots of screaming and shouting, and eventually a police siren. In my memory, though, the scene takes place in a vacuum, like in outer space. I remember the lights in the shop windows, the Christmas lights strung between the streetlights, the bridge to Lambertville with the headlights of cars on it, and the snow falling, falling from the sky like millions of little stars.

Then the sound all came rushing back, because Jack showed up. He was like an uncle to me, the guy she was going to marry the very next day. He'd been pressing her for years to get married. She finally agreed only a week before when he proposed on Christmas Eve in front of the whole family. They were planning a wedding for New Year's Day, to start the new millennium.

Now, everything was changed and Jack was devastated. He knelt next to her body and touched her cheek, and he sobbed because she was already getting cold.

He suddenly screamed, "God, no!" at the top of his lungs, and I went over and touched his shoulder. I'm not good with hugging, but somehow he responded to my touch. He got up slowly, like an old man, and hugged me tight. I stiffened, like I always do, but then I slowly put my arms around him.

"What was she doing out here?" he wailed. "Where was she going at midnight on New Year's Eve?"

CHAPTER THREE

I don't like funerals. I don't like all the crying, it gives me a bad headache. Plus, I just don't understand them. People cry and moan about the dead person, but there's nothing they can do to change things. I just sit there and think about how weird it is that we have to die. I don't get it how one minute you're there, and the next you're gone. It doesn't make sense to me.

It's like time. I don't understand it at all. Is it just a long chain of moments? If it is, then there are times when I want to just reach out and hold on to one of those moments, to take it in my hands and hold it up to the light and look at it from every possible angle. It's like how I'll take a note, or a series of notes, in a song and just play with it, examine it in detail. I'll go on for five, ten minutes just playing with that one phrase, seeing all the variations I can play on it, fooling around with the harmonics of it, changing the order of the notes and the time, and all sorts of other things.

I told you I'm different. Probably most people don't sit there in the pew at a funeral and think those thoughts, but I do.

There was a lot of music at Rosie's funeral. She loved to sing, and she had singer friends who came and sang the hymns at St. John The Evangelist Church in Lambertville. Afterward, there was a luncheon at the restaurant, and her friend The Dittybopper came. He was a DJ in the 1950s and 60s, and she'd worked for him at one time. He was a character, dressed like something out of the 1950s with sunglasses and a sharkskin suit and the fast-talking patter of a radio host, which is also what he'd been. He played doo-wop records at a turntable in the restaurant and told stories from his younger days, of acts and groups and record labels and a lot of behind the scenes stuff about the Mob.

My Dad took Rosie's death hard. The facts in our family are that Pete hardly knew his own father, who'd been a British naval officer that Rosie'd hooked up with in the 1940s, and besides, this man had died five years before. It had always been just Rosie and Pete, growing up, he told me. Of course, she left in the 1960s and spent ten years in England, a time that Pete still had a lot of bitterness about. He'd made up with Rosie in recent years, though, so at least there wasn't this big grudge between them still.

I like to look for patterns, and I think it's fascinating how families have their own patterns. Like, Rosie left Pete when he was young, and then Pete left our family when I was young. What he did was get mixed up in The Troubles in Northern Ireland, running guns to the IRA in the 1980s. He was involved with some dangerous people, and even when he was home he wasn't really present. He'd take calls at odd hours and disappear for days or weeks at a time, and when he was around he had a distracted air and a hair trigger temper, and he did not do a very good job as a father.

My brother Martin didn't remember as much about that, but I did, because I do not forget much. There was always a tension between Pete and me, and I tried to think of him as a father, but I was glad when I got old enough to move out. My mom was nice, but she and I were very different. The only person I felt close to was my grandmother Rosie, and it left a hole when she died.

After Rosie died I dropped out of school. I was supposed to be studying computers at Rutgers, but I lost interest in that. I told my parents I was dropping out for a semester, and getting a place near Rosie's restaurant, in New Hope. I didn't want to do anything but play music for a while, and Jack Caldwell told me I could keep playing at Rosie's bar, so that is what I did. Pete didn't like it, but he finally came around when my mom said it would be good for me to be there. Dad and I were arguing a lot, so maybe she wanted some peace in the house.

There was another reason that I wanted to spend more time at the restaurant. His name was Perry Lukens, and I couldn't stop thinking about him. I get stuck on things sometimes, and I was definitely stuck on Perry Lukens. I can't explain it, except that I thought we had a bond, something that connected us in a way I never connected with anyone else. It was like we understood each other perfectly. Or, at least I thought we did.

He was about six years older than me, still a young man, but he seemed like he was going places. He was different from most men his age. He was more focused, more intense. He was emotional, but somehow I understood his emotions, unlike I did with other people. I got a tingling in my stomach when I talked to him, and although I know now that can be a danger sign, I wasn't sure about it then. He seemed dangerous but very desirable, a Bad Boy who promised that every day would be a tightrope walk. I usually like predictable things, so it was new and exciting to be around somebody like him.

I remember the first time I saw him. I was in between sets at the bar, and I was coming back to the little stage after drinking a Coke at the bar (because I was still too young to drink legally), when all of a sudden this body appeared out of nowhere and walked straight into me. I stumbled and knocked into a waitress, who dropped a full tray of food on the floor. Luckily, nobody at the nearby tables got food spilled on them. I was irritated, though, and I got up and said, "You clumsy idiot, watch where you're going!"

I looked into eyes as deep blue as the morning sky, with black eyebrows and black hair. His gaze made me look away.

"I'm sorry," he said. "I'll help you up."

"Don't bother," I said, struggling to my feet. "You've done enough already." I got up and started trying to help the waitress collect the broken dishes, and pull myself together. He stood there anyway, and kept apologizing.

I noticed when we both stood up that he was right at my eye level. I'm 5'9" and I know I'm tall, but I don't usually like guys who are my size or shorter. He kept making eye contact, and although I tried to avoid his gaze, it made my stomach jump. He was looking at me like he had no fear, like he was brimming with confidence, and I liked that. He was like a bantam rooster, strutting around in a barnyard.

"Look, I told you I'm sorry," he said. "Can I make it up to you? Do they take that out of your pay? I'll pay for any damage. I can afford it."

He was wearing jeans and an open-necked white shirt that showed his sunburned neck. He must spend a lot of time outdoors, I thought.

"I told you, you've done enough," I snapped. "Just leave, will you?"

There are lots of times in my life when words tumble out of my mouth and I wish I hadn't said them, and that was one time. I did not really want him to leave, not at all, but there it was, the words were just hanging in the air between us. I just turned and left, because when you say something you should be prepared to act on it, and I had just said I didn't want to be around him.

I couldn't stop thinking about him, though, even when the other musicians and I started our set. I was playing the piano and I couldn't get lost in the music the way I usually did, because I kept looking at him out of the corner of my eye.

For the rest of the night I was really distracted, and I watched his every move. He was hanging out with some friends at the bar, and I studied him carefully. He strutted around like a rooster, but something about him reminded me of a scared little boy. I thought he was probably putting on a show for his friends, and it was pretty amazing that I could figure that out. Usually I couldn't figure people out that easily.

It was like there was a magnet across the room, and my eyes kept going back there. Every once in a while our eyes would meet, and I'd quickly look away, telling myself I wasn't going to look again, but it never worked. My gaze kept roaming to his section of the room.

At the end of the night I was sitting at the piano after our last set, when he came up and spoke to me. "Are you still mad at me?"

"I don't get mad," I said. "Anger is non-productive. I just got annoyed that you walked into me and made that waitress spill her tray. That wouldn't have happened if you had been paying attention. You should always pay attention in a crowded place like this."

"I told you I'm sorry," he said. "My name's Perry Lukens. I'm a builder. I do a lot of work on houses around here."

"What does that have to do with anything?" I said.

"I just thought you should know who I am," he said. "I'm not some clumsy loser who can't walk straight. I'm somebody!"

"I did not say you were a clumsy loser who cannot walk straight," I said.

"Well, I just wanted you to know those kinds of things don't usually happen to me," he said. "So, listen, can I walk you to your car?"

I never had a man ask a question like that before, and I was not sure what to do.

He kept looking at me.

"What's the matter?" he said.

"I don't know," I said.

He looked at me strangely. "Did you not understand my question?"

"No, I understood it."

"Well, can I? Walk you to your car?"

"I don't have a car," I said. "I live in an apartment a few blocks away. I walk home."

"Okay, well, can I walk you home?"

Certain expressions women use have always confused me, and one of them is, "My heart skipped a beat." I never understood how your heart could skip a beat because you were talking to a guy. Except, right then, my heart skipped a beat.

CHAPTER FOUR

"I live in town," I said. "I'm just a few streets away, down near the river. You can walk me there if you want."

It was April 5, 2000, at 12:25 AM, and even though there was still a chill in the air left over from winter, it was not too cold for walking to my apartment. The sky was clear and there were hardly any cars at this hour. We walked along the river and looked at the streetlights reflecting off the moving water, and it was very peaceful. I could get lost looking at the patterns the light made on the surface of the river, so I had to force myself not to look at it.

Perry did most of the talking. He asked a lot of questions about my grandmother, my family, and New Hope. He said he was new in town, and he was still getting to know his way around.

"I like it here, though," he said. "I'm from a place called Ironton, in southeastern Ohio, a little town just across the Ohio River from Kentucky. It's an okay place, but everybody knows everybody else, and my family was looked down on. My Dad couldn't ever seem to hang on to a job, because he had a lot of bad habits and no good ones. He spent some time in jail because he stole things. We got by, but I wanted more. Hell, I was born wanting more. I came to Philadelphia in high school, on a bus trip to see the Liberty Bell and all those historic sites, and I decided then and there I was going to move here when I got older. There's more action here. You don't feel like the world is passing you by."

He had big plans, he told me. He wanted to be a millionaire before he was 30, and he said he was on his way to that. "I worked seven years in Ohio doing construction, and then I moved here. I got a job with a home remodeling company, and I worked for them for a couple of years, keeping my eyes and ears open, learning everything I could. I always knew I'd go out on my own eventually, though. So I started talking to the customers, asking them if they needed any odd jobs done, that I'd do them on the side for a better price."

"So you were taking business away from your company?" I said.

He looked at me and his eyes were blazing and he stuck his chin out. "Damn right," he said. "That's what you have to do. It's just what you do to make it in this world. Nobody's going to hand you things, Rosalie. You have to reach out and take them."

"Didn't your company find out?"

"Oh, yeah, they finally did. The boss called me into his office one day and said I was fired. Said he'd make sure I never got a job with another remodeler. But I didn't care. I knew enough then to start my own company. I had money saved to buy my own tools, and I had contacts, people I'd been bringing along for years. I went out and bought my first truck, and by the next day I was bidding on jobs. I've been making money since the first week, and now I have two other guys working for me. I'm a comer!"

We were walking along the low stone wall by the river, and Perry stopped suddenly. He looked across the river at New Jersey. "You know, there's a lot of potential for a guy like me here," he said. "There's lots of land just waiting to be developed, houses to be built. I have ideas, Rosalie, big ideas. I can see my name on a lot of properties over there, and here too. I'm going to be a player in the real estate business around here."

It was big talk, and I thought it was amusing that he made

17

statements like that. I know people call that a Napoleon complex, when a short man gets all puffed up and acts like he's king of the world, but there was something about this Perry Lukens I couldn't resist. He had a sense of newness about him, a sense that he really was going places, and I found it intriguing. I wanted believe him when he said, "You watch me. You'll be hearing about Perry Lukens for years to come in this town. Believe it."

I am not much for poetry or romantic scenes, but I think you should pay attention when something out of the ordinary happens. Like, just then, just as he said that, I am not lying but there was a shooting star. It flashed across the sky in an instant, and left a tail that didn't fade for a few more seconds. I know it was just a pebble falling into the Earth's atmosphere, nothing supernatural at all, but it somehow made that moment special. And Perry must have felt the same way, because he suddenly moved close to me and kissed me.

I have never really liked the idea of kissing, and the reality hadn't happened to me up to this point in my life. I don't like touching, or any kind of close contact with people, and that's probably why I had never had a boyfriend. I figured things would always be that way, and I had accepted that I would probably never have a close relationship with a man.

But Perry grabbed me so fast that I didn't have time to move away, and before I knew it he had me pressed up against the stone wall and was kissing me hard. It was confusing and weird and disgusting and yet also very magnetic. I wanted it to continue, although at the same time I didn't.

My heart was pounding and I heard all kinds of voices in my head, and it seemed like there was music playing somewhere, and there were lights flashing -- it was like I was in another universe for a minute there.

Finally I pushed him away, and he looked at me with those flashing eyes and seemed to look right into my soul. He was breathing heavily and his face looked flushed, although I turned my head away quickly.

"I'm sorry," he said. "I shouldn't have done that."

We walked the rest of the way to my apartment in silence. My apartment was only a few blocks away, and in no time we were there. I knew better than to let him come upstairs, even though I sensed that he wanted to. We stood by the front door for long minutes while he started talking about his life goals, and then I said, "Well, I should be going. I had a long night and I'm tired."

"You sure I can't come in?" he said. "We could talk some more."

"No," I said. "I don't think that would be a good idea."

"Well, can I kiss you?" he said. He moved an inch in front of my face when he said that, and it startled me so much I took a step backward and started to topple off the step. He reached out and grabbed me and I felt the surprising strength in his arms. It shouldn't have surprised me, since he looked wiry and strong and sunburnt and outdoorsy, but it did. There was one crazy moment when I thought he was going to kiss me, and then I pushed him away again.

"No," I said. "I don't like kissing."

"I'm sorry," he said. "I screwed up again, didn't I?"

"No," I said. "It's me. I'm just like that. I don't like getting too close to people."

He shrugged. "Well, that makes two of us. Of course, I know I have to deal with people if I want to get ahead. I'm shy, though, really shy, and it's an effort for me. I can understand where you're coming from."

"No, you can't," I said. "I'm not shy. I'm probably autistic or something. It's just the way I am. Most people don't understand it. You probably don't either."

"No, I don't," he said. "I don't even know what that word means. But that doesn't matter; I still think you're special. I'd like to see you again, if you don't mind."

I had never had anyone say that to me, and it took me by surprise. "I have to think about that," I said.

"Oh, okay," he said, kind of deflated.

"Yes," I said. "You can see me again." I leaned over and kissed him on the forehead, and then I went in the door and closed it behind me.

CHAPTER FIVE

The date when Perry kissed me was April 5, 2000 at 12:53 AM. I told you before I like to remember dates. Time fascinates me, which is probably why I like jazz. It's all about improvising, but you have to stay within the form. You have a definite time to get your notes in, and that's it. You can play around a lot in that structure, though. You can develop themes, patterns, play with the beat and the melody, but you have to always come back, you can't ignore the fact of time. What's strange is that there are occasions when I am really wrapped up in what I'm doing, playing with all those patterns and tonal colors in the music, and I'll just lose track of time. I'm in this state where there's no time, I'm just suspended in a dreamlike place without time or space. That's eternity, I guess.

Sorry, I get carried away sometimes and lose my place in the story. It's just the way my mind works.

Anyway, as the spring of 2000 progressed, I spent more time with Perry. I wanted to keep seeing him, but the whole thing seemed dangerous and unpredictable too. I had never had a boyfriend, and it was something so new.

There was something about him that was different than other people, something that made him connect with me. I don't know why, but he understood me more than other people. And I understood him, everything about him.

Like, the huge hole in him where his confidence should have been. I saw through all his big talk, his bragging and strutting around, and I could see there was a little boy in there. He was afraid of being a nobody, of not having anyone care about him, and that's why he was so driven to make a success of himself. He thought that was the only way to make people notice him.

But because of that he would do anything to achieve success, and he didn't really trust anyone. I knew that it wasn't a good idea to trust Perry Lukens, but I couldn't help myself. I know, you're thinking how stupid could you be, Rosalie, getting together with a guy you don't trust? Isn't that a recipe for disaster? Well, in my family we do that a lot. We're always skating on the edge of the thin ice, and once in awhile it breaks and we get wet and cold and almost die of pneumonia.

But then we dry off and warm up and go out and do it again.

It was the strangest thing. Every time I was around Perry, I had two completely contradictory voices in my head: one was a high-pitched, moaning sound, like some old woman singing a wordless Blues. It was a warning sound, but it also had a grieving, hurting tone to it. It was the sound of trouble coming, I knew.

The other was a young man's voice, a man in the peak of his youth and confidence, a voice with an Irish lilt to it. "What a blazing great day," it said. "Why, anything could happen!"

I guess the young man's voice won out.

It was exciting to be around Perry, and I fell in love with that. He had more life, more juice, more force, than anyone I'd ever met. He was determined to live every day hitting on all cylinders, he had what they call a lust for life, and I never met anyone who made you feel more alive just by being around him. I mean, he woke up every day and he was ON, he was going to climb up that ladder and wring every ounce of whatever it was he wanted out of life every day, or he'd die trying. He was ALIVE, that's what it was.

And maybe I needed that, seeing as how I was still trying to process the death of my grandmother. I had experienced the utter randomness of Life up close, and I was confused and shocked by it. I needed something or somebody to jolt me back to a different way of thinking, to convince me that Life went on like the river I could see from my apartment window, and that it wasn't going to stop just because I needed time to sort things out.

So that's probably why I ignored the alarm bells. Perry and I spent a lot of time together that spring. He would come by the restaurant after work, and I was always glad to see him. I would sense the little bubble of his ego coming in the door, and I saw him strutting up to the bar like a peacock, and my heart would just do a flip, every time.

We didn't go out much. Perry told me he was saving his money, and he couldn't afford to take me out except to cheap little pizza joints and places like that. The reason he came in the bar every night was because he wanted to be seen. There were important people there, he said, and he wanted them to know who he was.

"I'm building my reputation," he said, "and I need to be seen. All the money people in the area come here to hang out after work. I want them to see me as a player, and this is the way. To mingle with them, show them I'm for real."

He was determined to make it. It was so obvious in the way he walked and talked, even I could see it. He would take me on long walks at night and tell me his plans. It was always what he was going to do, what he planned to accomplish, nothing about me. I sometimes wondered if he knew anything besides the most basic details of my life.

Jack Caldwell, who was still overseeing the Skibbereen

23

Hotel after Rosie died, didn't like Perry. "Why are you seeing that runt?" he'd say. "I don't trust him. There's talk he undermined his boss at the last job he had. You shouldn't trust him, he looks like he'd trample over anyone who got in his way." I didn't pay it any mind, but one day Jack Caldwell made his concerns clearer to me. He pulled me aside one day at the restaurant and said, "I told you I don't like that guy you're seeing. Do your parents know about him?"

"No they don't," I said. "But I'm an adult, Jack, and I can make my own decisions."

It was June 6 of 2000, at 5:20 PM, and we were sitting on the little deck that overlooked the river, and I could see scullers in the late afternoon sun.

Jack looked older these last few months. Rosie had been the love of his life, and her passing had devastated him. He was wearing his favorite black leather jacket, but it looked too big for him now; he'd lost weight and he looked thin and small.

"Look," he said. "I know you're an adult, and I don't want to butt into your business, but I feel protective toward you. Rosie always felt close to you, I know that. I don't want to see you hurt. I did some research on this guy, looked him up in some databases I have access to, and he's had some lawsuits that were brought against him because of shoddy work, overcharging people, etc. He doesn't have a great reputation."

"I appreciate that you want to look after me, Jack," I said, "but I'll thank you to stay out of my business. I don't care what you found out about Perry. I like him, and that's enough for me. I don't need you doing background checks on my boyfriends. Now, if you don't have any other nosy things to say, I have to go."

24

I walked off without saying goodbye to him. I feel bad about it now, because Jack was an old man who was just trying to do right by me, but what can I say, I can be a stubborn person sometimes, and nobody was going to change my mind.

That night was a turning point in our relationship, because I decided I wanted to sleep with Perry. He had been trying to get me in bed for months, and I'd resisted, but there was something about his insistence, his full speed ahead charge that changed my mind.

But I wasn't interested in having sex with him. That's not something I do. I just can't picture that in my head, not even a little bit. I don't like touching, which I told you before, and sex is all about touching. I know what people do when they have sex, but it's just one of those things that separates me from other people. I thought I'd spend my life alone because of that, but Perry didn't seem to mind.

He understood when I told him. "That's all right," he said. "It's a hornet's nest for me too, Rosalie. I never did understand why somebody would want to open themselves up that way. I can't relax enough to just let go, I guess. This just proves you and me are made for each other, don't you think?"

We were in his little house in the hills above Lambertville, decorated in early Wal-Mart. It was nothing special, really, but it felt like home to me. Perry had a bed that was really just a mattress on the floor, and for meals we just ate pizza and candy, which was all he had. When it got dark we drank bottles of soda and sat up talking for hours and hours, watching the sun come up over the mountain, and for the first time in my life I felt happy.

CHAPTER SIX

The funny thing was, that was the night -- June 6, 2000 -- that I started getting these weird dreams. I've always thought in patterns, and my dreams have been the same way. They're mostly just patterns of colors or sounds, and although I enjoy them, they never surprise me or teach me anything new.

But that night I had a very strange dream, not like anything I ever had before. It wasn't just random stretches of color or sound, it was a story, and I could remember every detail when I woke up. It was like a movie that I could replay anytime I wanted, and it was always the same. It was strangely intense, more real than my day-to-day life, if you can understand that.

Anyway, it went like this. I was standing at the bottom of a green mountain, and it was a beautiful spring day. The sky was deep blue with streaks of clouds sweeping by, and I could feel the sun on my face, and the breeze was ruffling the wildflowers on the side of the mountain. I knew there was something I was supposed to see on the top of the mountain, and so I started up a path. The path wound around the side of the mountain, and sometimes I was on the side that faced the sea, and the higher I got the further out I could see, till near the top there was a wide expanse of blue ocean that stretched all the way to the horizon, many miles away. I could see whales far out, some of them breaching the ocean in magnificent leaps, while hundreds of others swam in pods, till the water was foamy from the movement of their great bodies. I could hear music, a heavenly music, and a kind of chanting that got louder as I neared the top of the mountain.

When I got to the top I saw a little stone house, and the

chanting seemed to come from there. It was hardly big enough for an adult to stand up in, and I hesitated at the front door. Before I could knock, a little man came out. He was about four feet tall with a gray green smock on and black shoes with buckles and a red pointed hat. He didn't seem surprised that I was there.

"What are they saying?" I asked, wanting to know what the chanting meant.

He didn't answer; just put his finger to his mouth and then motioned for me to look in the door.

I bent down and looked in, and I could see a little wooden table with chairs, a stone fireplace, and some other furniture. The little man motioned for me to wait, and he went inside for a moment. When he came out again he was holding a piece of paper. He gave it to me, and when I looked there were four numbers written on it: 8765.

"What is this?" I asked.

He smiled, revealing a row of small white teeth. At that, the chanting stopped, the scene disappeared, and I woke up shaking. I could see the blue glow of Perry's clock radio across the room, and the numbers said 3:00.

I must have been shaking so much that I disturbed Perry. "What's the matter?" he said, sitting up in the bed. "Did you have a bad dream?"

"I don't know what it was," I said, "but I can't stop shaking." I was so upset that I didn't mind him putting his arms around me. I needed him to be close to me and I was glad he was there. "It was really strange. It seemed so real, though. I actually thought. . . " I looked down at my hand, expecting to see the paper with the numbers on it, but it was gone.

Perry asked me a lot of questions about the dream, but then I didn't want to talk about it. "I don't know what it means," I kept saying. "I've never had a dream like that before."

I told him I wanted to go back to sleep, but I couldn't get back to sleep for a long time after that. It wasn't just that the dream was so vivid; it was that I couldn't shake the feeling that I belonged there. It seemed like a part of me lived there, if you can believe that. It seemed like going home, somehow, and I felt like the paper was a present, a sign of that. It was puzzling, mysterious, and I couldn't get it out of my head.

The next day I still couldn't shake the dream, and I went around all day with the images and the sounds in my head. By this time in my life I had taught myself how to do graphic design on my computer, and I was starting to get some freelance jobs designing Web sites. I would go to go to a little coffee shop with my laptop computer and hang out every day, designing Web sites till it was time to go to my job playing music at the restaurant.

I was friends with the owner of the coffee shop, a woman named Myra. That day when I told her about my dream with the numbers, she said, "It sounds like you dreamed a lottery ticket number. You should buy that number, maybe it will win."

"No thanks," I said. "I don't like to gamble."

I don't understand gambling, actually. I don't understand why people would want to bet on something just because they have a feeling they'll win. When you look at the odds of winning the lottery, they are so steep that you have an infinitesimal chance of winning. Still, I did have something, a little voice in my head, I guess you'd call it, which seemed to think there was a message in that dream.

I put it out of my head, though, and just went about my business, and I forgot about it.

The next day I went to Myra's coffee shop, and as soon as I walked in the door, she said, "Did you buy that ticket?"

"I told you I don't like to gamble," I said.

"Well, the number won," she said.

I had to sit down. "What do you mean?" I said.

"Just what I said. The number you dreamed won. It was the winning Pick 4 number last night."

So, June 8, 2000, at 10:00 AM was when I knew that something really strange and unexplainable had happened to me. I told Perry about what happened, and he looked at me with an odd light in his eyes.

"You should develop that skill, babe," he said that night over pizza at his house. "It could make you a lot of money."

"It was just luck," I said. "Or, just some weird dream that came out of the blue. It'll never happen again."

"No, I bet it will," he said. "Next time you see numbers like that in a dream, buy the lottery ticket yourself. Don't go throwing something like that away. Somebody else won on that number, and it could have been you."

"It was just a one-off, I'm sure. I won't get a dream like that again."

But I did. I got one a couple of weeks later, and it was just as strange as the first one. I wasn't at Perry's house this time; I was sleeping in my own bed in my apartment. It started out with music, a strange music I could hear before I could see anything. It was like no music I'd ever heard, played on instruments I'd never encountered, and it sounded like it was coming from a place far away.

I gradually realized I was outside, and the music was blending in with the sound of a rushing stream. I was standing next to it, and I could see smooth white stones in the bottom of the stream bed. I could hear the music playing on a hillside behind me, like a ragtag band of musicians was marching along playing their instruments. I wanted to turn around and see where the music was coming from, but something told me to look into the stream. There, I noticed the stones had arranged themselves into four distinct groups. There were three pebbles, then two, then a group of six, then three again -- 3263. It was all so clear and vivid, just like the last dream.

I woke up in a sweat, disoriented, and lost. I reached next to me in the bed for Perry, but he wasn't there. It took me minutes to realize that I was in my own apartment. I sat up trembling, and padded out to the kitchen and poured myself a glass of water. The light from my microwave said 3:00 exactly, just like before. It was all too weird, and I had the impression that something, some force or other, was in the apartment with me. I switched on every light, sat down at my kitchen table, and called Perry.

"It's me," I said, when he answered. "I had another dream."

"Rosalie?" he said groggily. "What time is it?"

"It's 3:00 in the morning. Just like the last time. Perry, I don't like this."

"Why? It's just a dream. And it could be a very good dream. One that can make you some money."

"I don't like it. These dreams are like no dreams I've ever had. They're weird. They're disturbing. And, listen, I really felt this time that something else was here."

"Something else? What do you mean?"

"I feel like something is in my apartment watching me."

"You just got spooked, babe, that's all. Just go back to sleep, I'm sure everything's okay."

"No," I said, shivering. "It feels real. Like something's here."

"I'll be right over," he said.

That was the good thing about Perry. He was all about himself, and he measured everything in the world by how it affected him, and sometimes I wondered how much he cared for me, but other times he was someone you could depend on. And he could be forceful, which I needed right now.

He came over and spent hours sitting with me on the couch, and I finally fell asleep in his arms. The next morning, though, he was determined that I should buy a lottery ticket.

"You know it's going to win, like the last one," he said. "You have to do it. Come on, Rosalie, if you don't buy one I will."

We were sitting at my little kitchen table drinking coffee. Perry always got up before dawn, ready to start climbing his mountains each day, and he would wolf down a bagel with cream cheese and some cereal. His energy level, always high, was highest in the morning. It was like he couldn't wait to put his plan for world domination in motion every day.

"I don't know if I want to buy a ticket," I said. "I don't think I want to win the lottery."

He thumped the table with his fist. "Are you kidding me? Why wouldn't you want to win the lottery?"

"I don't like this psychic stuff. I mean, I always had minor psychic stuff going on, like hearing strange music sometimes, but this is different. I never had dreams like this before. I don't want that, Perry. It's too much. Things aren't supposed to work like that. People aren't supposed to dream the winning numbers of lottery tickets."

"Why not?" he said. "Maybe you're special. Didn't you tell me once you're descended from Irish witches?"

"Oh, that's just something my grandmother told me. She didn't know if it was true. She had no idea. She just said the women in the family had some psychic ability, and that was her explanation for it. It's just something to laugh about. I never expected that it would be like this."

He put down his coffee cup and stared at me. "This could be a gift, Rosalie. A gift that sets you apart from other people. You have to find out if it's true. All I know is, nobody ever gave me anything like that in my life, I've had to work for everything I got. If a gift dropped in my lap like that, I'd know what to do with it."

"I'm sure you would," I said, refilling his cup. "But I'm not you. I don't want this in my life. It's too much responsibility."

He looked at me like I had two heads. "Sometimes I don't understand you, Rosalie, I really don't." He pushed his chair back from the table and stood up. "But I can't waste any more time. I have to get out to a job and make sure my guys aren't stealing from me. I'll see you tonight." He kissed me on the top of my head and left, and I sat there wondering what to do.

I read this book once called "The Origin Of Consciousness In the Breakdown Of The Bicameral Mind", and the author, a guy named Julian Jaynes, had this hypothesis that the right and left lobes of the human brain used to be divided into a speaking part and a listening part. He thought that primitive people "heard" their gods and spirits talking to them, but it was really the right brain speaking to the left. Jaynes thought that something happened around 3000 BC that caused an evolutionary shift and created modern consciousness, where the two sides of our brains are more fully integrated and we don't experience those auditory hallucinations.

Sometimes I think maybe my brain is like one of those older brains, and that the voices and the music I hear are just my right brain communicating with my left. I mean, where was it all coming from? I don't like to think there are supernatural reasons for this stuff, so the lottery dreams shook me up. If I could dream winning lottery tickets, what else was in store for me?

I'd rather not think about things like that. My usual practice is to put those thoughts out of my mind, try to forget them. I don't like uncertainty, don't like when you can't figure things out. I don't like unanswered questions.

But, in the end, I had to find out the answer. Did I dream a winning number again?

When I stopped into the coffee shop that morning I went up to the counter and bought a ticket from Myra. I bought one with the number 3263.

I promptly put it in the pocket of my jeans and forgot about it. I didn't really want to think about it much; it was too hard to figure out. I went about my business that day and put the ticket out of my mind, but when I went to the Skibbereen Hotel late in the day to get ready for my music gig, Perry reminded me.

He was standing at the bar when I walked over to him at the end of my set.

"Well?" he said. "Did you buy the ticket?"

"Yes," I said, putting my hand in my pocket to make sure it was still there. "I bought it this morning."

"Good," he said. "Let's have dinner at your place and we'll watch the lottery drawing on TV."

We bought a pizza and took it home to my apartment, and watched the news while we waited for the drawing at 7:00.

Perry was so excited he couldn't sit still. He kept pacing around the apartment, and he said he felt like he was ready to jump out of his skin. I've always thought that was a strange expression, by the way. How can you jump out of your skin?

Finally, the lottery drawing came on, and when it came time for them to draw the Pick 4 number, Perry was so nervous his leg was twitching. We watched as the little balls lined up, one by one, and when the last one appeared, Perry shouted so loud I thought the whole town could hear him. It said 3263.

"This is amazing!" Perry said. "I never believed in that psychic bullshit, I thought it was all just a big con job, but there must be something to it. You have some kind of gift, Rosalie, that's for sure. This could be a big thing for us."

"What do you mean?" I said.

"Well, isn't it obvious? You could win the big one sometime. This Pick 4 is just small change -- $2500. All you need is one of those dreams to give you the winning number for the big payout, and you're on easy street. You won't have to work for the rest of your life! They have jackpots in the hundreds of millions, babe. We'll be set forever."

I shuddered. "How do you know I'll ever get a dream like that? So far the prizes have only been worth a few thousand dollars. It's a long way from $100 million."

"I know, but it could happen. You could get a dream like that."

"I don't want a dream like that."

"For God's sake, why?"

"It upsets my ideas about reality. It turns my world upside down. It's just too strange, that's all."

"Man, I don't understand you, Rosalie." He came over and sat next to me on the couch, then cupped my chin in his hand and tilted my face so I could look at him.

35

"If you don't want it for yourself, want it for me. I'm out here scrapping every day, trying to build something, and sometimes I feel like I'm never going to make it. It's hard, Rosalie, when you're a young guy trying to get a foothold here. I'm always trying to convince all these snobby realtors and bankers and moneymen that I have what it takes, and they look at me like I'm some low class hick from Ohio who's dumb as a post. I have to make it, babe, or this life isn't worth living for me. If you don't want to win that money for yourself, win it for me. I could use it to expand my business. Maybe I could start buying houses and fixing them up, then reselling them for a profit. That's what I'd really like to do. You've got to help me out, Rosalie."

He was holding my chin and I had to look at him. I could see the hurt in his eyes. I never felt like I could understand anyone before, but it was so clear to me that he was like a lost little boy with a world of hurt inside him.

"Okay," I said. "The next time I get a dream like that, I'll let you buy the ticket."

CHAPTER SEVEN

It wasn't easy to dream the number of a winning lottery ticket, though. It was something I had no control over, although Perry didn't seem to believe that.

He asked me every morning: "Anything happen yet? Did you get one of those dreams last night?" He always looked disappointed when I said no.

Maybe I didn't get a dream because I didn't want one. I don't know, but the fact is I didn't have any dreams for months and months.

I went about my life and forgot about the dreams after awhile. Or, if I did think of them, I was starting to accept them as mere coincidences, just pure dumb luck. So then it became ordinary, in the way that any random, magical, unexplainable event starts to lose its sparkle, and it begins to seem more ordinary as time goes on. Sometimes I think that's what must have happened to at least some of the people who were around Jesus, because, really, how is it possible that only a small group of his followers realized he was something special? There must have been lots of other people who saw him do amazing things, but they just found a way to fit the miracles into their day-to-day lives. "Oh, raising Lazarus from the dead? Nothing special, really. Yeah, I saw it happen, but I still had my bunions and my indigestion, and everything went back to normal pretty quickly."

I think when miracles, or whatever you want to call them, happen they seem extraordinary for about a day, and then people just go on with their lives. Miracles start to seem less like miracles with every passing day.

That's what happened with my lottery dreams; after a while I didn't even think about them anymore.

Until one night, I had one again.

Maybe I wanted it, in a way. Perry had lost out on some bids lately, and his work had slowed down. He was looking thin and haggard with worry, and he had this haunted look. He was starting to doubt himself, and it was not pretty. He was one of those men who were born to be cocky, and when he couldn't play that role it was like seeing a bird that couldn't fly. He was like a peacock that couldn't display its feathers or make that brassy call that peacocks do to announce themselves to the world, and instead just went mute. He stopped bragging, stopped telling me all his plans for conquering the real estate world. He needed something to change soon.

So at 3:00 in the morning of February 14, 2001, I got a dream again. This time I was walking up the mountain and it was like the angels were singing me along. I heard a choir of many voices singing in some strange language, the voices ranging from whispery high notes at the top of the register, to deep, groaning bass notes at the bottom. I got to the top of the mountain and sitting by the little stone house was the most beautiful girl I'd ever seen. She had long blonde hair cascading down her back and she was wearing a long white dress that was belted with a cord of silver. She was sitting on a wooden chair and talking to a small boy with golden hair. The boy looked at me and smiled, and ran away. I thought the girl would go running after him, but instead she turned to me and spoke. I didn't see her lips move, but I heard her anyway.

"Do you want to know?" she said, holding out her hand to me. Her fingers were closed into a fist, and somehow I knew if she opened the hand there would be the numbers for a lottery ticket. She wanted me to answer, so that there would be no doubt.

"Yes," I said.

She opened up her hand and there was a small white bird in it. The bird opened its mouth and I heard the number "4491".

I woke up sweating and trembling. I knew this number would win a lot of money. I got up without waking Perry and I went to the window and looked outside. It was winter, and the sky was dead clear, with the stars like chips of ice in a black void. I wondered if my life would change because of this dream, but I knew I had to give the number to Perry.

I told him at breakfast. He was drinking his coffee, and he almost spilled it when I said, "I had one of those dreams."

His eyes lit up immediately. "You mean, one of those dreams, those ones where you see a number?"

"Yes," I said, shivering. "I saw a number."

He put his coffee cup down loudly. "All right! This is our lucky day, babe. Gonna win big tonight!"

"I don't want to buy the ticket," I said. "I don't feel good about it."

He frowned. "Don't want to buy the ticket? Are you crazy? What are you going to do, just let somebody else win it?"

I looked away. "No. You can buy it. I just don't want to."

He could hardly contain his happiness, but he tried to appear calm. "Are you sure, babe? I mean, you're the one who dreamed it. You'd let me buy it? That's really nice of you."

"Yes, I'm sure. I don't want to buy it. You do it."

He almost bolted out of the apartment, in his hurry to get downstairs and find the nearest convenience store that sold lottery tickets.

He ran away so fast it troubled me. I wanted him to stay and talk about this strange dream with me, but he couldn't wait to buy that ticket.

He needs a boost, I told myself. He's gotten a lot of bad breaks, and he needs something good. Maybe this is just my gift to him.

That evening the ticket won, and it didn't seem unnatural at this point. The dream had been so real to me that I knew for sure the number would win. This time it won big, though. It was for $100,000, and Perry was so excited when we saw the numbers come up on TV that I thought he was going to have a heart attack. His face got red, and his mouth was gaping like a fish sucking air when you pull it out of the water. His hands were even trembling.

"This is the most wonderful thing that's ever happened to me," he said, tears filling his eyes. He got down on his knees in front of me. "I promise you, Rosalie, I will use this money for good. I will not disappoint you. I will do good things with it."

I guess I was stupid for giving the number to Perry. I've done plenty of things that seem stupid by other peoples' standards. I don't see things the same as other people, and I make decisions that don't seem right to them. I know that most women would not give a

$100,000 gift like that to a guy, especially one as self-centered as Perry Lukens. I mean, I didn't realize till he went home that night that it was Valentine's Day, and he hadn't even bought me roses.

Then again, Valentine's Day has never meant much to me. I don't look at the world like other people, and I don't do things that people expect me to do.

The dreams, though, they rattled me. I didn't like getting messages from another dimension, or wherever they were coming from. It gave me the creepiest feeling, and I didn't want any part of it. Besides, something inside me said I wasn't supposed to profit from the dreams. I don't know how I knew it, but I did. The knowledge I got from the dreams was something I was supposed to give away to someone who needed it. And Perry had such a gaping need for it, that I just said, "Here, take it."

Perry didn't waste any time. The day that he brought home the check for the winnings, he was happier than I'd ever seen him, and he had so many plans.

"You know that old Victorian house I told you about?" he said. "The one outside of town that has the foreclosure notice on it? There's an auction in a week, and I'm going to bid on it. I'll get that place cheap, fix it up real good, and sell it for a profit. I'm on my way, babe!"

His bid won at the auction, and he got the house. By April 6, 2001 he was working on it full time, usually at night after he was finished his day jobs. He'd pack sandwiches and coffee, and he'd work till 4:00 in the morning, then come home, shower and sleep for an hour before getting up to go to his regular jobs.

Perry was good at what he did. He knew how to do beautiful

41

carpentry, and he could figure out most other jobs that needed to be done in an old house. I would sometimes go with him at night and watch him work, and it was the only time he seemed really calm. He was very methodical about measuring and fitting things together, and he would get so lost in his work that he seemed in another world. I understood that, because when I'm playing music or working on the computer I'm the same way.

Perry was obsessed, and he barely noticed 9/11 when it happened. I couldn't stop looking at the images of the burning buildings on September 11, 2001, but Perry came home only long enough to eat a quick dinner, and then he went back to work on his house.

I guess I should have known from that incident that Perry was so focused he wasn't going to let anything get in his way, but I already knew that. There just wasn't much room in his head for other people, but I understood that. I'm pretty much the same way, or at least I thought so then. I looked at Perry and me as people who had a bond, and maybe it wasn't love, but it was better than anything I'd had up till then.

Perry finished the job on September 19, 2001, and he sold the house for double what he paid for it. Now he was on his way. He bought two more old houses quickly, worked on them through the winter, and sold them in the spring, making another good profit. The old cockiness was back, and he had a smile on his face all the time now. He was starting to get some respect in the local real estate community, and he was getting invited out to dinner by people who'd never given him the time of day before.

"I got plans, Rosalie, big plans," he'd say. "I'm talking to people now who can really make them happen. Bankers. Real estate investors. They're looking at me differently now, like I could be a player. It's all going to come true!"

I didn't have any more of those strange dreams, but Perry didn't need them now. He had the money behind him, and he was going places. Things were moving so fast it almost seemed like our life was a dream, when I look back on it.

I went back to school for a semester a few months later, and this time I took Accounting. I've always been good with numbers, and Perry said he needed me to help with the bookkeeping. He didn't trust anyone else to do it, so he asked me to take care of it. It seemed like he needed me more and more, because he kept asking me to handle more and more of the administrative work. That was fine with me, because I liked working with numbers more than dealing with people. I even quit the little jazz combo I was playing with, because I got tired of having to talk to the other guys in the band.

But my most important function, Perry said, was to be his good luck charm. He trusted my judgment and he thought somehow I was connected with some inner wisdom, even if I wasn't aware of it, and so he talked to me about a lot of his decisions. I should say he talked his ideas out loud to me -- the most important voice to him was always his own.

Perry did always take me to look at houses he was thinking of buying, because he thought I had some kind of mojo that would help him make the right decision.

"You know, Rosalie," he'd say. "I don't know how you do it, but you're always right. I wouldn't do a deal without you by my side."

Things were really starting to break for him, it was true. Perry was like a surfer riding a wave, and he was on a high every day. He woke up with a fire in his eyes, and he just couldn't wait to get out of bed and get started on his day. He'd call me all day long and tell me what was going on, and his voice was always full of excitement. "You'll never guess what happened!" was his favorite expression, and he sometimes seemed like he was dancing with nervous energy while he was talking to me.

At night he wanted to take me out with him to meet the important people he was dealing with, but I usually said no. I don't like meeting new people as a rule, because I don't know how to make small talk, or say things to make them like me. Instead, I listened when Perry came back and told me who he met and what they talked about, and then we went over the numbers involved in his deals. He trusted me to keep him up to date on how much money he had in the bank, when his bills were coming due, all the money stuff.

Lots of times at night we'd end up in one of the houses he was rehabbing and I'd help him while he installed an appliance or fixed something, or finished a floor or painted a room, or any one of hundreds of other jobs he could do. He couldn't get the jobs done fast enough, and it seemed like our lives were speeding up by the day.

My parents didn't like Perry, I have to say. Dad thought he had a questionable moral character, and Mom thought he was too self-centered.

It was so exciting to be part of something that was growing every day, though. Perry rented office space in New Hope, and I set up shop there with a desk and a computer. I was a jack-of-all-trades

-- I did the books, I answered the phone, I paid the bills, I designed the advertising and marketing materials -- every day I was busy.

My Dad kept warning me not to put my name on any legal documents that would mean I had a share in the business, but I knew that wasn't going to happen anyway. Perry loved me, as much as he could love anyone, but he wasn't going to split the profits of his business with me.

Maybe that's what saved me in the end. But the time for that is later, years later.

There were so many good years in between. Did I say good? They were great, exciting, Fourth of July and Christmas morning all wrapped up in one. It just seemed like everything we touched turned to gold, like we could do no wrong. It was a time when money was loose, and the bankers seemed like they wanted everybody to have some. "Here, you want some money to buy a house? Oh, you have sketchy credit? No problem, no problem at all. We can overlook all that, those loans you defaulted on, the late payments, the patchy job history. No need to stop the party -- come on, just sign the papers and we'll be happy to give you carloads of money!"

That's what it was like. Perry got a reputation as a guy on the move, a guy who was going places, and the bankers and real estate guys jumped on his back and let him carry them. They were eager to help him make bigger and bigger deals all the time. By January 1, 2005, Perry had 35 guys working for him, and he owned his own real estate -- a couple of apartment buildings, some commercial buildings, some houses here and there. By 2006 he was up to 50 workers, and now Perry owned a bar and even a little hotel in Stockton, New Jersey. He was working constantly, and so was I, and the money was rolling in.

My Dad still didn't like him, but he seemed impressed by his work ethic, if nothing else. "That guy is all about himself," he'd say, "but at least he's not letting any grass grow under his feet. He's a worker. I just don't know how long he can keep it going."

I remember one night when we were staying in a room on the third floor of the hotel he'd bought, and there was a little balcony that looked out on the river. It was September 25, 2006 and the leaves were starting to change colors, but there was still a warmth in the air remaining from summer. We had just eaten a dinner of smoked salmon, broccoli, and fresh fruit for dessert, and Perry had opened a bottle of champagne to celebrate finishing work on an apartment building he'd bought in Lambertville. He was in a happy mood, and he looked out at the river for a long time.

"Sometimes it's hard for me to believe, that I've come this far so fast," he said.

"It's been a great ride," I said.

"I couldn't have done it without you, Rosalie," he said.

I was surprised. He didn't usually thank me, so anytime he did it was special. I raised my glass and said, "To your business, Perry."

"To us," he said, touching my glass.

Then he reached across the table and said, "I got this for you."

It was a little blue box. I opened it, and there was a diamond ring inside.

"What's this?" I said.

"Will you marry me?" he said. "I want to marry you, Rosalie. I want to be with you the rest of my life. I want you to share in my triumphs. We'll have a family together. We'll go from one success to another. What do you think? It'll be a great ride."

CHAPTER EIGHT

I looked at my watch and saw that it was 7:17 PM. I did that so I could remember the moment, because I did not know if anyone would ever propose marriage to me again, and I wanted to remember that on September 25, 2006 at 7:17 PM, somebody did.

Then, I closed the box and handed it back to him. "No," I said.

I glanced at his face, and it was twisted into a frown. It looked like he was not happy with my answer. "What do you mean?" he said. "Don't you love me? Why wouldn't you want to marry me?"

I took a long time to collect my thoughts. "I don't know if I understand love," I said. "I enjoy spending time with you very much. It's fun to see all these great things happening for you. And I've never felt this close to anyone before."

"Then why won't you marry me?" he said. He fidgeted around in his seat, opening and closing his hands like he had too much energy and did not know what to do with it.

"I don't think I am ready to get married," I said. "It's not you, it's me." That was true, but there was something else. It was hard to put into words, but I just thought we would not have a good future together. I knew Perry was selfish, and he did not think about other people very much, but then again, I could sometimes be the same way. I don't understand people, and I usually prefer my own company. I did not think that the way I was and the way Perry was would make a good match.

"I still don't understand," Perry said. "You're 26, aren't you? That's old enough. I'm in my 30s, Rosalie, and I should be married. People take you more seriously when you're married."

"I can't explain," I said. "I just don't think I'm ready. Why don't we keep things the way they are? I'm not the right person for you to marry, Perry. I'm not good with people, and I would not be what you need. Let's just have fun for now, and see where things take us. Maybe I will be ready later."

"Okay," he said, putting the box in his pocket. "That's fine, but I don't like it when people don't take my offers, Rosalie. And just remember, if you wait too long, I might not be here."

He got up and left, slamming the door behind him.

I sat there for a long time, watching the stars come out in the night sky. I know the names of all the constellations, but I often wonder why people chose those particular patterns and made up those particular names. I like to see other patterns in the sky and make up my own names sometimes.

Life is about patterns, I think. You can see patterns if you look for them. And in fact the pattern of Perry and me breaking up started that night. Looking back, it was easy to see that night was the start of it.

Oh, you could choose a different date, I suppose. Things really started to go wrong around the spring of 2007. But the seeds of it were all on that late September night.

It seemed to get cold right after that, and it never really warmed up again. It was a gray, sleety kind of winter, with a lot of those days when the sky doesn't seem to be able to make up its mind if it is going to snow, or sleet, or dump freezing rain, or just hold off. Perry's business always slowed down some in the dead of winter, and it was a time when he did a lot of his brooding and dreaming up new conquests to make when the weather got warm. We'd spend a lot of time at the coffee shop down the street from the office. Sometimes Perry would meet with his banker, a guy named Blake Elden, and they'd drive around and look at properties, go over his finances, gossip about local business deals, and talk about business. They met for lunch almost every day in the winter, and lots of times Perry brought Blake back to the office.

"How's the money girl?" Blake would say, when he saw me. He always wanted to joke around, but I never laughed. I just did not think he was funny, that was all.

I guess I did not trust him. He was always so friendly, but he seemed to be trying too hard to be friends with Perry and me. Like, he would call me, "Rosie Babe".

"My name is Rosalie," I told him one day. "Not Rosie. Rosie was my grandmother."

"Right, right!" he said. "I remember her. Shame what happened, that drunk driver killing her. I was there, you know."

I didn't remember him being there the night my grandmother was killed, but I let it pass.

I decided that Blake was coming around so much because he was like a gambler betting on a horse. I don't gamble, but I met some gamblers one summer in high school when I worked at a racetrack. I've always loved animals, so one year my parents got me a job at this track in New Jersey. I just worked in the stables, mostly, feeding the horses and cleaning up after them, but sometimes I would see men hanging around and watching the horses when they worked out. One of the stable hands told me they were gamblers, and they liked to keep up on certain horses, just keep their eye on them to see how they were doing. I thought Blake was doing that with Perry, keeping an eye on him to see what kind of shape he was in.

I told Perry that one night and he laughed. "Well, maybe I am like a horse to him. That's because he knows I'm a comer, and he's just backing me. He's been real helpful in getting me the money I need to keep buying properties and expanding, and it's making him look good with his bosses. I'm one of the biggest customers his office has now, did you know that? Me, Perry Lukens, I'm a big commercial customer now." He seemed very pleased with that.

"He is not your friend," I said. "He is just betting on you to win. I just hope he is not talking you into anything dishonest."

Perry laughed and shook his head like I was a little child. "Babe, what am I going to do with you? Everybody is dishonest in business. Honesty doesn't get you anywhere. All these guys out here, all the movers and shakers, they're not telling the whole truth. I mean, they ain't outright lying; they're just shading the truth. They're putting things in the best possible light. Making everything look pretty, that's all. It's the way you get ahead. Blake is no different than the rest of them."

"Well, he's not your friend, that's all," I said. "I just don't want to see anything bad happen to you."

"Don't you worry about it, babe," he said. "He's just a part of my team. There's nothing to worry about."

But things were coming apart right then and I did not see it.

Looking back on the sequence of things, I see that I got signs. I was getting dreams again, but not the kind like before, with beautiful mountain scenes and choirs of heavenly voices. No, these were nightmares; there was no other word for it. I was always trapped in a cave somewhere, or lost in a dark forest, or on a boat in the middle of the ocean with dark clouds fast approaching.

It was never clear what was going to happen, it was just something bad. I woke up screaming sometimes, covered in sweat, so disoriented I didn't know who or what I was. Perry had to hold me tight and stroke my hair and whisper in my ear to get me to calm down. "It's all right babe," he'd say. "Don't worry, everything'll be all right."

When I calmed down enough to talk about it, I'd tell him. I kept wondering what the dreams meant, but Perry said not to pay attention to them.

"Things are going so good," he'd say. "I don't see how anything could go wrong. I got more work that I can handle, and my investments are making money every day."

"Maybe you should put everything on hold," I said. "Stop moving forward all the time."

He laughed. "You must be joking, right? I got a payroll to meet, babe, and I'm mortgaged to my eyeballs. If I stop for a minute the whole house of cards will fall down. I'm like one of them sharks that has to keep swimming or I'll die."

I did the books, so I knew he was right. He was making money, but he kept borrowing more all the time, and he couldn't just walk away from it, or everything would collapse.

So, I let him convince me, and I stopped taking the dreams so seriously. And what happened, of course, is that the dreams stopped coming. When you don't pay attention to the voices, they stop speaking to you.

But that doesn't mean the problem went away.

CHAPTER NINE

In the spring I like to watch for hawks. The red-tailed hawk is common in Pennsylvania, and I like to watch them. I love to see them circling high up in the sky, riding the air currents and thermal updrafts, just flapping their wings ever so slowly to adjust their flight. They glide around up there and look for field mice, rabbits, or voles. They look like they're just floating along lazily, but when they see something they swoop down to investigate. They have amazing vision -- I've read that they can see the ultraviolet spectrum, and they can even sense polarized light and the Earth's magnetic fields. When a hawk sees a small animal in the grass far below, it swoops down and kills it with its claws. I think they are majestic birds, and I can look at them for hours.

The spring is the time when the real estate market is supposed to heat up, but the in the spring of 2007 it never happened. Perry started to get anxious about it. He'd come to the office sometimes in the afternoon and say, "Not much happening out there. Nobody's bidding on anything. Blake says the foreclosure rate has gone up, and people aren't as willing to buy. I'm sure it's just a temporary thing, though." He acted like he was not concerned, but I could hear the tension in his voice.

And things did not get better. When May came, and then June, and Perry wasn't getting any offers on the houses he had for sale, I told him the company's bank account was getting low. He decided to take out a loan to meet some expenses. In the past he always had renovation jobs that would provide him with income, but they had dried up too. Nobody was calling to have him quote on jobs. He was letting his workers go home early some days, because he didn't have anything for them to do.

I started getting phone calls from suppliers with overdue bills, and I didn't like dealing with them. Sometimes I wouldn't answer the phone, and I'd just leave the office and walk down by the river, searching the sky for hawks.

Then on June 14, 2007, at 11:15 AM Blake Elden stopped by the office when Perry was out.

"Hey, there, Rosie, how's it going?" he said, talking very loudly, like we were friends.

"It's Rosalie," I said, hardly looking up from my computer. "And it's going lousy. And Perry isn't here."

"I know he's not," Blake said, sitting down across from me. "I came to see you, honey."

"Well, that's a first," I said. "You've never come in this office and asked to see me. What can I do for you?"

"I need to ask a favor," he said. "I know you handle some of the bookkeeping for this outfit, and I want to ask if you can see your way to making a payment on some of Perry's loans. He's got that line of credit, you know, and a few mortgages, and he's been falling behind. I'd talk to him about it, but I know you're the moneybags around here. He probably doesn't know much about what's going on with the financial end."

"No he doesn't," I said, "but that's not because I don't try to tell him. Every day I try to talk to him about it, but he doesn't want to listen. He thinks everything will be okay, that's what he tells me all the time."

Blake cleared his throat. "Yeah, I know, he tells me that too.

55

And it's great to be optimistic, I'm all for that, you know. It's just, it's just, he needs to make a few payments to give him some breathing room. To give us some breathing room!" He was drumming his fingers on the desk, and I noticed he was bouncing his leg up and down.

"Did you have too much coffee?" I said.

"No," he said. "Listen, Rosalie, I'll put it to you straight. I went out on a limb for Perry. I got him more money than he probably should have gotten, based on the fact that I believed in him. I went to bat for him, you understand? I figured he was a good horse to bet on, if you know what I mean. I mean, the kid is hard working, ambitious, he dreams big. And he made some good bets himself, on properties in the last few years. He's been making some healthy profits, right?"

"I don't know," I said. "You should talk to him about this. All I know is that none of his properties are selling."

"You don't have to tell me that," he said. "I know it very well. Nothing's selling anywhere right now. Foreclosures are up, and the bank is taking a hit on all these loans that aren't getting paid. People are talking about a real estate bubble, that properties have been overvalued for awhile now, and there's a correction coming. Hell, maybe it's already here."

"I hope not," I said. "It would be bad for Perry if that happens."

"He's not the only one!" he snorted. "It's bad news for everybody, me included. Listen, I can't have this happen right now. I bought some investment properties myself, went in a little to far, I guess, but the point is, I'm mortgaged to the hilt myself. Perry is my biggest client. If things go bad for him, and I lose my job. . ." he shuddered. "All I can say is, I'm going to be in big trouble if that happens. I have a family, Rosalie, and I live in a big goddamned house, my kids are going to expensive schools, we belong to a country club -- all that takes money, and it's going to fall apart if I'm out of work."

"Don't you have any savings?" I said. "Even the animals know to put food away for the lean times."

He looked at me like I was insane. "Savings? What's that? I haven't saved a dime in ten years. I'm living beyond my means, Rosalie, just like everybody else in this part of the country. If a crash comes, there's going to be a lot of blood in the water."

"I can't help you," I said. "You should talk to Perry about this. I'm just the bookkeeper."

He reached across the desk and touched my arm, but I pulled it away. "Don't do that!" I said. "I don't like people touching me."

"Okay," Blake said. "But, please, Rosalie, try to get him to understand how serious this is. I'm not going to tell him how to run his business, but he's got to find a way to come up with that money, or it's going to be bad for all of us."

"I'll talk to him," I said. "I'll try to get him to listen."

"Thanks." He got up and walked out, and I looked at him closely for the first time and noticed his shoulders were sagging like he was carrying a big weight on them.

That night I tried to talk some reason into Perry. We took a walk along the river, one of our old haunts, although things had been so busy for the last year that we hardly ever got the chance anymore. But tonight the stars were out, it was a clear, balmy night, and there was a big yellow moon hanging just above the trees. I was waiting for the right time to bring up the subject of Blake's conversation, when Perry suddenly got very excited.

"I got a call today from my Mom," he said, suddenly.

He never talked much about his mother, and I didn't even know if the woman was dead or alive, so I was surprised to hear about a phone call.

"What was it about?" I said.

"She's coming out to see me," Perry said. "In two weeks, over the Fourth of July weekend."

"That's nice. Any special reason?"

"She's coming to check up on me, I know. Oh, she said it was just a visit, but she never does anything like that. I've been living here for almost ten years, and she never came to visit before. It's because I sent her a newspaper clipping about the hotel, when I bought it six months ago. She used to be a cook in a hotel kitchen. She thinks she knows everything about hotels. She's just coming out to inspect, look over my shoulder and make sure I'm not screwing up."

"Maybe she's proud of you," I said.

He laughed, but it was that kind of laugh where there's no humor involved. "What would make you say that? I told you, she never bothered to come in ten years. No, she can't believe I'm doing well enough to buy a hotel. She told me all the time when I was a kid that I was a screwup, and that I'd never amount to anything. She's just coming out to make sure she was right about that. Well, I'll show her. I told her we'll put her up in the best room in the hotel, and she won't have to pay for a thing while she's here. I'm going to show her I made it, Rosalie. She's going to leave here thinking her boy is the most successful businessman in Pennsylvania!"

His eyes narrowed and his jaw set the way it did when his stubborn streak appeared. I knew it wasn't going to be easy to bring up finances now, but I had to.

"Listen, Perry, I'm glad your mother is coming, but spending a lot of money to impress her isn't a good idea right now. Blake Elden stopped by the office today, and he was asking that you come up with some money to pay down some of the balances on your loans."

"So?" he said. "Just write some checks and pay him."

I sighed. "No, Perry. I've been trying to tell you for months, but you never listen. The company finances are not good. We have a lot of bills, and I'm late on the mortgage payments. You have all those unsold properties right now, and even the renters in your apartment buildings are taking longer to pay us. I don't know what's going on with the economy, but things are not looking good. You need to cut costs, Perry, not add to them. I think you'd better start thinking about laying off some of your workers."

"I'm not laying off anybody!" he said, and I could see the veins in his neck throbbing, he was so angry. "I didn't work this hard all these years to finally make it, and then have it slip away. These guys look up to me, Rosalie. It's the first time anybody in my life has ever looked up to me, and I'm not going to let them down.

Things will get better, just you watch."

That was the last time that I got a chance to talk to Perry about money. He just would not talk about it anytime I brought it up after that. We started bickering, and he got cold and withdrawn. I started sleeping at my own apartment again, and I spent less time at his house.

In the daytime, at the office, he closed his mind to any talk about business. Even when Blake Elden showed up -- he would just change the subject, or sometimes he wouldn't even come in the office if he saw Blake's car parked outside. All he wanted to talk about was his mother's visit.

Perry wanted to put the best show, to do everything first class for his mother, and he wouldn't think of pinching pennies in any way.

"I'm going to make this a special time for her," he said. "So she can go back and tell all the folks at home how good I'm doing."

His mother showed up in a beat up old Chevy with 200,000 miles on it but she acted as if it was a Porsche and she was a queen. I didn't look at her too closely, but I could tell she didn't smile much. Her voice was high and screechy, and it hurt my ears. She asked Perry why I didn't look at her, and Perry just said, "Oh, that's just Rosalie. She doesn't look at people."

"Well, she seems odd," his mother said.

I didn't get upset, because I'm used to people thinking I'm odd. I decided, though, that I wasn't going to spend any more time around her than I had to. I did not think anything I could do would change her opinion of me.

But then, she did not seem to think much of Perry, either. She never once praised him, and in fact she was much more likely to criticize whatever he told her. No matter what Perry said or did, no matter how much he bragged about the size of his company, all the projects he'd worked on, or how much his properties were worth, his mother, whose name was Addie, barely raised an eyebrow. Perry gave her the best room in the hotel, a suite on the top floor that looked out over a scenic stretch of the Delaware River, and he wouldn't allow Addie to pay for so much as a cup of coffee, but I never heard her thank him even once.

I could see that it must have been difficult to grow up with her as a mother. She seemed to think she was an expert on cooking, and she was free with her opinions about every meal that she ate. The hotel kitchen seemed to annoy her in particular.

"Damn salad isn't fresh," she screeched, one night. "And that's not all. The meat is tough and it's overcooked. My steak tastes like shoe leather. No wonder you don't have any customers in your dining room, boy. You ought to fire that chef pronto. He's ruining your business."

I didn't think Perry was listening, but the next day he came into the office and said, "You can write out a check for wages for the chef at the hotel. I fired him this morning."

"Why?" I said.

"Because my mother is right, he's a lousy chef. I need somebody there who knows how to run a kitchen. That dining room is losing money, and I'm going to turn it around. Make it the place to go in the area for a great dinner."

"But now you have to hire a new chef," I said.

"My mom said she'll help me," Perry said. It did not sound like a good idea to me, but he insisted. I guess he wanted to feel close to his mother, and he thought that would be the way to do it.

But it didn't work, because a few days later Addie announced she was going back home. "I don't like the East," she said. "Too many evil people here. I don't like the way the women dress, and I don't like what I see on TV, and I don't like the way the people talk. There's no religion here. You'd do well, Perry, to move back too. This place is bad for you."

Perry was standing by his desk looking through some mail when she walked in the office and made that announcement, and he didn't say anything, but I could tell by the way his hand shook that he was upset by it. He really wanted his mother's trip to go well, but now it was all falling apart.

Addie left and at first I thought it would be good, because now Perry could concentrate on business, but that did not happen. He took a long time to hire a new chef, and when he did it was a man who turned out to be incompetent, and within a month the hotel dining room had fewer customers than before, which added to all the other problems.

And then Perry started to drink too much.

At first he was just staying out after work and coming home hours later reeking of whiskey. He would tell me he was meeting with important people, but he'd never drunk this much before. He got even more short-tempered when he was drunk, and he'd often pick a fight with me. I knew what was happening; he was feeling pressure from all sides, and he didn't know how to deal with it.

Then I found out he was cheating on me.

CHAPTER TEN

I don't understand cheating at all. First of all, that word "cheating" gives you an idea of what's wrong with it. You're supposed to follow the rules in life. Cheating means you're not following the rules.

And besides, I think that when you find something in life that works for you, you should stick with it. I don't understand why people would look for something different. I don't like change, myself. Change makes me uncomfortable.

For some reason, though, Perry decided to cheat. He was supposed to be my boyfriend, but he decided to have sex with the wife of Blake Elden.

Her name was Margo, and I'd seen her before when we went to various functions. When things were going well Perry was getting invited to a lot of those kinds of events. Blake's bank sponsored a 5k run for charity, and Perry and I ran in it. Margo was there, in her pink and mauve running outfit, and I saw her smiling and laughing with Perry, but I didn't pay it any mind. I thought she did that with everyone, the toothy smile and the winking, and the hugging, all of it.

I don't know why she would want to break the rules, either. She had two small children, and a nice life with Blake Elden. They lived in a big house with lots of ground around it, and a pool in the back. Blake and Margo had invited us to the pool a few times, and I thought it must be nice to live in that big house. It was a very ordered, neat house with everything in its place. I loved the library, where Blake had rows and rows of books all in alphabetical order.

The kitchen, too, had everything sorted and put in its place -- the counter was spotless and the pantry had everything sorted into different shelves. It looked like the interior of a house from one of those glossy magazines about interior design.

One thing about Margo, though, it seemed like she liked to categorize people, and I was in the category of stupid. She talked to me like I was a child, and I always thought she was making jokes that I couldn't understand. Generally I can handle that, because I've had lots of people in my life who have treated me like I'm stupid. I don't argue with them, I just go along and do what I do. Usually they find out eventually that I'm pretty smart about certain things, but if they never catch on I don't get upset about it.

It was after Perry and I started spending more time apart that it happened. I was only spending one or two nights a week with Perry now, and even at that, there were times that he left me sitting alone for hours while he went out drinking with his buddies.

Or at least I thought that's what he was doing.

Looking back, I guess I should have seen it coming. Things were tense between me and Perry, because he just wouldn't listen to reason about the money. I'm not a financial genius, but I can see when things are heading for disaster, and I was trying to warn him. He just acted like I was nagging him endlessly, and every discussion with him about it turned into an argument. It was like he was driving a car straight off the edge of a cliff but he refused to believe his own eyes. All the signs were there: he was out there every day trying to drum up business, but people weren't returning his phone calls, or when they did talk to him they said they were "reevaluating" and they'd get back to him. And that was just the people who'd been talking about doing a deal. The work he already had wasn't going well -- several of his projects got put on hold or cancelled, and each time he lost another job he'd go out that night and get drunk.

Then he started bothering me about the dreams. He'd come home drunk and say, "How come you don't have any more of those dreams, Rosalie? We could sure use one now. What's the matter, did your gift go away?"

"I can't make the dreams come," I'd say. "If I could, I'd dream up another winning lottery ticket, you know that. It's just not something I can do."

"If you loved me, you'd have a dream for me, babe," he said one night. He was sitting on the couch looking tired and beaten down. He was haggard these days, and he had a bruise on his cheek from a bar fight he'd gotten into the week before. His hands were dirty, his hair was messed up, and he had on an old pair of work jeans with a hole in the knee. He didn't look like a master builder, that was for sure.

But when I tried to sit next to him and talk like we used to, he pushed me away. "I don't need that," he said, roughly. "What I need is one of your dreams, honey, to turn this mess around. Can't you just call one of them up? I need it bad."

I told him again that I had no control over it. I tried to explain, but he just went to the refrigerator and got out another beer, then turned on the TV. It was like he'd shut a door, and I was on the other side.

I could have handled that, I guess, but the cheating with Margo, that's what pushed everything over the edge. It was just a bad time, that's all. My Dad and I weren't getting along, because he kept reminding me that he didn't like Perry, and every time Perry and I had a fight or things took a turn for the worse, he'd bring it up again. I felt like I was alone in the world.

Then it got even worse. My Dad had his own computer consulting business, and he was doing some work for the bank where Blake Elden worked. Apparently Margo came in one day, dressed to the nines, looking like something out of a fashion magazine, and Dad must have asked a question or two about who this creature was. One of the bank employees told him who she was, and while she was at it she filled him in on the latest gossip, that Margo had been seen coming out of a certain hotel with Perry Lukens, and that she'd planted a big kiss on his mouth before she got into her car.

So of course my Dad called me with that news, and it was the last thing I wanted to hear. Before he could start lecturing me I hung up.

I guess I always knew inside that Perry would do this some day. I knew he had it in him, and I knew it was going to happen eventually. Perry really only had one person he cared about deeply -- himself. He always felt that he needed to watch out for himself, because nobody else would.

It bothers me when I don't know the answer to an important question. I like to figure things out, and then I can go on with my life. So, I decided to see for myself if Perry and Margo were cheating. I decided to go to the hotel and find out.

I needed to see it with my own eyes.

CHAPTER ELEVEN

I planned it carefully. I started reading through Perry's emails, for one thing. Perry was never much of a computer guy, and he'd only started using email a year before when I told him it was good for business. I designed a Web site for him around that time, and I thought it was important for Perry to personally answer the emails that came in. He complained about it, and I had to just about drag him to the computer to make him do it.

That was until about six weeks before, when all of a sudden he seemed much more interested in checking his email. Sometimes he'd come into the office during the day and check it, and I just thought he'd finally accepted the fact that he had to communicate this way with customers.

That is until I checked his inbox and saw messages from Margo. She'd been sending him messages for quite a while, and it was pretty easy to see that they were fooling around. She called him, "Hammer and Nails," and she wrote lots of syrupy messages about how he could build a new house for her anytime. Perry's emails were not nearly as wordy -- usually, he was just telling her where he'd meet her next. I could follow the progress of their relationship, it was all there.

And I knew they were going to meet again. They had met every Wednesday night in Room 206 at the hotel, and so I decided I'd pay them a visit the next time.

So, on October 17, 2007, a Wednesday night, I got the expected phone call from Perry, telling me he needed to meet with some customers, and he'd be back late. "Don't wait up," he said. "I don't know when I'll be home."

It's really hard for me to lie, and I didn't want to let him know I knew what he was doing, so I just said, "Okay," and hung up.

It was 7:06 PM when Perry called. I waited till 9:00 PM before I went to catch him. I chose that time because I knew they were meeting at the hotel at 7:30 PM, and I figured they'd be pretty well along by then.

So at 9:00 PM I drove over the bridge to New Jersey and then I made my way to the little town of Stockton. I parked my car around the block from the hotel and then I got out and walked down the street and through the front door. I was lucky because there was nobody at the front desk. The front desk person, a young woman with black hair, purple lips, and pasty white skin looked up as I came in and it seemed like she recognized me as Perry's friend.

"Can I help you?" she said, in a high, nervous voice.

"Yes," I said. "I'm here to see Perry Lukens."

"I can't do that," she stammered. "I, I don't know who you are."

"Yes you do," I said. "I work for Perry. I need to see him now. Please give me the key."

She fumbled around underneath the counter, and gave me the plastic card to open the door of the room.

"I don't want any trouble," she said. "It's Room 206."

"There won't be any trouble," I said, walking over to the

elevator and pushing the button. I don't know why I said that. I had no idea if there would be trouble or not.

When I got off the elevator at the second floor I saw there was a repeating pattern in the carpet. The carpet was a rose color with turquoise squares and each one had a black diamond shape in the middle of it. There were three rows of these squares going down the hallway. I counted 27 seven in the middle row by the time I got to Room 206.

The door to Room 206 was a pale blue color, and there was a little gouge halfway up the door where it looked like somebody had dented the door with something heavy. It was probably from the cleaning cart, or maybe from somebody moving furniture into the room.

I notice things like that all the time. Details. I get lost in them sometimes.

I slipped the card into the lock, heard it click, and then I pushed the door open.

I didn't see anything at first because the shades were pulled down and the room was dark. Then my eyes adjusted, and I saw where the bedroom door was. I noticed clothing strewn all over the floor -- Perry's pants, a pair of black high heels and a blue dress. There were also several empty beer bottles on the coffee table by the TV. I walked over to the bedroom door and pushed it open.

And inside I immediately knew something was wrong. It looked like a storm had passed through. There was furniture overturned, the sheets, coverlet and pillows strewn about the floor, a lamp knocked over, and blood everywhere.

Perry was sitting on the floor near the bed, his face in his hands.

His bloody hands.

I didn't see Margo at first.

"Perry," I said. "What happened? What's going on?"

He looked up at me, but it was like he didn't recognize me.

I knelt down next to him. "Perry, it's me. Rosalie. What happened? Where's Margo?"

At the mention of her name he seemed to come around. He blinked and then focused, and seemed to recognize me.

"Rosalie? What are you doing here?"

"I read your emails, Perry. I know what's been going on. I know all of it. Where's Margo?"

He put his head in his hands again. "What a mess. Everything is falling apart."

"What's wrong?" I said. "What happened? Where is she?"

His face went blank again, and he mumbled something I could not hear. I shook him. "Perry. Maybe I can help. Where is she?"

He pointed to the other side of the bed, and I stood up and went around and I saw her.

She was lying face up on the floor, covered in blood from

70

scratch marks everywhere, and her head was twisted at a crazy angle. Her face was puffy and red, and her eyes were staring wildly.

At nothing.

I touched her wrist, but there was no pulse. She was dead.

I suddenly felt sick and a wave of dizziness came over me. I sat down on the edge of the bed.

I couldn't speak for awhile, but then I shouted, "Perry, what happened? What did you do?"

He didn't answer, so I got up and went around the bed and got on the floor and slapped him, hard, across the face. It was like some raw energy rose up in me and made me do it, and I was shocked for a moment after it happened.

Perry didn't even flinch. It was like he couldn't feel it.

"What did you do? Tell me!" I said, finally.

"I don't know," he said. "I can't, I don't. . .". He was trying to talk, but he was not making any sense. He seemed like he was in a daze. I could smell beer on him, and his eyes were blurry. I shook him again and finally he focused.

"I don't know, I'm confused. I, ah, I was seeing her on the side. I'm sorry, Rosalie. It just happened, I don't know how, I kept seeing her around town and she was friendly and things weren't going well between you and me, and. . ."

"It's okay," I snapped. "I know about what you were doing, Perry. That is not what I'm asking. What happened here? What happened to her?"

He put his head back against the wall and closed his eyes, and let out a deep sigh. "I don't know, it was like, like something came over me. I had some beers while I was waiting for her, and then she came and we, well, she was like a tiger. She ripped off my clothes, and I did the same to her. We were like wild animals, we couldn't get enough of each other."

I guess some women would not like to hear their boyfriend talking about having sex with someone else, but I did not get wrapped up in it. I just wanted to know the facts, so I carried on. "Okay, I get that. But how did it go from that to this?" I said, pointing to where Margo's body lay.

"Honest, Rosalie, I don't know. Everything is a blur. We had a crazy relationship. It was just bizarre. It got violent before, you know. She didn't like normal sex. I mean, we barely ever talked. It was crazy, just pure sex. I never had anything like that. She liked me to put my hands around her neck, and," he stopped and put his head in his hands, unable to go on.

I shook him again. "Okay, I understand about all that. I don't know why you would get involved with somebody like that. Pretty stupid if you ask me, but then the whole thing is stupid. Having an affair with the wife of your banker? That's not very smart, Perry. But I still can't understand how you got from something that was just stupid to this mess. You need to focus fast and tell me what happened, because this situation isn't going to go away. What happened?"

"I told you, it got physical," he whined. "She was pushing me all the time for more, more, more, to take more chances and do rougher things. I just went along with it, because I enjoyed the sex. But this time something snapped. She kept calling me a loser, a stupid construction worker, and a lot of other stuff. It turned her on to get me mad like that. I had my hands around her neck and this anger, this stinking anger, just came over me and I tightened my grip -- oh, God, Rosalie, I can't believe this happened! It was like the blink of an eye, and all of a sudden it was over. I'm so scared, so scared!"

I am not good at reading people, but even I could tell that Perry was afraid. He looked lost and confused. I guess some women would have hugged him now, but I don't do that. Instead, I just patted his shoulder and said, "Let me think about this a minute."

But there was nothing to think about. My boyfriend had just murdered someone, the wife of a local banker, and he had done it after a session of sex in a hotel room.

And now I was involved, because I came in just after it happened.

Suddenly I thought I heard a voice. It was a man's tenor voice with a strong Irish accent. "Run!" it said. "Get away, get away, get away."

The voice was clear and strong, and it echoed in my ears. My chest felt tight. Get away. That's what I should do. Just run, run away from this situation. Maybe Perry and I could just walk out of the hotel, get into his truck and run. Drive far away, maybe to Mexico or South America. Someplace where nobody would know us. We could disappear; just vanish into the crowds in a faraway city.

I looked at him. He was scared, and shattered looking, and he had blood all over him, but I could probably get him cleaned up enough and calmed down enough to get out of here without the desk clerk noticing anything. We'd have a few hours, maybe, until Margo's body was discovered, and then maybe a few more before the story hit the news and the police started looking for us.

"Darlin' get away!" the voice said again.

"What are we going to do?" Perry said.

I got up. I was going to do it. I was going to leave with Perry.

But then something made me look at the body again, and I knew I couldn't do it. It was impossible. A life had been snuffed out, and I couldn't run from that. I couldn't let Perry run either.

"We have to call the police," I said. "Right now."

His eyes got wide. "No! I'm not calling the cops. No, no, no!"

I bent down to him. "Perry, we have to. You can't run from this. And now I'm involved. If I let you run away, I'm part of it."

He was like a caged animal. "No! I'm not doing that. My whole life, everything I've worked for, it'll all be gone. I ain't going to prison, Rosalie. I saw what happened to my Dad when he went away. It ruins everything. I been trying my whole life to be different, be better than him. I wanted to be better than that shitty life I came from. I'm not going to the cops!"

"Perry, it's the only way," I said. "What are you going to do, pretend it didn't happen? People around here know you were messing around with Margo. When her body is found, you'll be the prime suspect. And what about the girl downstairs at the desk? She

74

saw both of you, she knows what's been going on, I'm sure."

He stood up and paced the room. "There must be a way. People get away with all kinds of stuff. There must be. I'll just leave. I'll get in the truck and go. I'll have to leave all this behind, everything I worked so hard for" -- here his voice cracked -- "but I'll get over it. I'll go someplace far away and start fresh. I'll change my name, grow a beard or cut my hair different, something to make me look different. And I'll just start fresh."

He looked at me, wanting me to agree. I couldn't do it.

"It's not going to work," I said. "They can trace you through your bank card, Perry. I mean, what are you going to use for money? How are you going to start a new life? They'll trace you through your Social Security number, your driver's license, your credit cards. They have lots of ways. They'll put your picture on TV, and in all the Post Offices."

"I'll leave the country," he said. "I'll go to South America. Or, Canada. Or, I don't know, France or something."

"Oh, I can just see you in France, trying to build houses. Or, are you going to do something totally different, like drive race cars? Come on, Perry, you know it's not going to work. We have to go to the police."

"No!" he shouted, and for just a split second, he looked like something completely different, a different being than the Perry I knew. He startled me, and I took a step backward. He saw my reaction, and he struggled to get control of himself. He put his hand against the wall as if to brace himself, and he waited till he got himself calmed down.

"There has to be a way," he said, finally, his voice almost a whisper. "I can't face up to this, babe. I have to find a solution, because otherwise. . ." his voice trailed off.

I went over to him and touched his arm, the way I did sometimes when he wanted to be touched. He suddenly put his head on my shoulder and started weeping. I did not know what to do; he had never done anything like that before. Finally, I just started stroking his hair awkwardly until he calmed down.

When he finally stopped crying, I said, "Trust me, Perry, it will be all right. Now, just sit down on the bed and I'll call the police. I'll handle everything."

He sat on the floor again, looking dazed, and I went to the beige phone by the bed and picked it up. I pushed #9 to get an outside line, and I dialed 911.

"Hello," a voice said. "This is 911. Do you have an emergency?"

I turned to look at Perry, and he was holding a knife in his right hand, and he was about to slit his left wrist.

I dropped the phone, and it clattered to the floor. "Hello?" I heard the voice on the other end. "Hello?"

I knocked the knife out of Perry's hand and slapped him again. "What are you doing?"

He looked up at me, and I saw how serious he was. He was really going to slit his wrists rather than go to prison.

"I can't face this," he said. "Let me go, Rosalie. Save

yourself. I'm not going."

I decided then that I couldn't let him go. I was going to have to break the rules, and it bothered me, but I couldn't watch him kill himself.

"Come on," I said, pulling him up from the bed. "Come on, we're getting out of here."

I could still hear the voice on the other end of the line saying "Hello? Do you need help?" as I quickly bundled Perry out of the room, and hustled him down the hall to the elevator.

CHAPTER TWELVE

There are times in my life when I wish I was invisible, and this was one of them. People think that chameleons are the best animals at changing color to match their environment, but there are half a dozen other animals that are better, including octopus, squid, and various lizards and frogs. I've always wanted to just blend in with the background wherever I am, but of course, humans can't do that.

I don't really like being the object of attention. I don't know how women can stand having men look at them when they walk down the street. I don't like it at all, and that's why I usually don't wear anything to make me stand out from the crowd. I don't like the feeling of being noticed.

That is not a good trait to have when you're running from a crime, of course, because then you start to worry that everyone is noticing you.

The first challenge was to get past the young woman at the front desk of the hotel, and that's when I really wanted to be invisible. I had no idea what to say if she talked to Perry and me, and I was actually shaking as we rode down in the elevator.

When the elevator door opened I took a deep breath and stepped out, just hoping the girl at the desk would be distracted.

I was in luck, because she wasn't even standing at the desk. She must have stepped into the office for a minute, or maybe she'd gone to the bathroom, but I was just glad she wasn't there. In fact, nobody was in the lobby at all, and I hustled Perry right through it and out the front door.

Out on the street, I felt like everybody was watching us at first, but then I realized there was hardly anybody around. It was 10:05 on a weekday night, and the street was mostly empty.

"Where's the truck, Perry?" I said. "Where did you park it?"

"It's around the corner," he said. "On Boyer Street, by the alley."

I made for the corner, then we took a left and went to the end of the next block, and halfway down the one after that. The truck was parked under a tree by an alley. We hadn't passed anyone walking, and I was grateful when I finally got Perry in the passenger door and then I went around and got in the driver's seat.

"Where are we going?" Perry said, handing me the keys. He was in a daze, but he kept wringing his hands over and over.

I did not know where we were going. I just wanted to go somewhere away from here. I turned the ignition on, put the truck into gear, and just drove. I drove through the back streets till I somehow found my way to the bridge leading to New Hope, and then I went along the river road, just trying to get somewhere I could stop and think for a few minutes.

I guess at a time like that your mind looks for familiar things, because before I knew it I was driving up the winding road leading to my parent's place. They lived on the side of a steep hill, and you could not see their house from the road. Everything was hidden by trees, and at night it was very dark and remote -- you could have been in the middle of a vast forest in Canada for all you knew. I drove up the gravel driveway to the house, when I got there I screeched to a stop, kicking up stones everywhere, and I got Perry out and hustled him inside.

The house was wood shingled with a porch and three stories, and it was surrounded by almost five acres of trees and rocks and a small stream running down the side of the hill. Inside I could hear a TV tuned to a sitcom, and I saw my mother in the kitchen. She looked up and smiled to see me, but her smile immediately froze on her face.

"What's wrong, Rosalie?" she said. "You look upset."

"I will explain everything in a minute," I said. "Can Perry use the bathroom? He needs to clean up."

"Sure," she said. "You know where it is, right Perry?"

"Go," I said to Perry, pushing him in the direction of the stairs. "Use the one upstairs. Down the hall to the left, in case you forgot. Mom, where is Dad? I need to talk to him."

"He's downstairs in the den," she said. "Watching his favorite show. What's the matter?"

I went over and grabbed her by the arm. "Come downstairs with me and I'll explain to both of you."

Dad was sitting in front of the TV on the couch, and he got up to greet me. "This is a surprise," he said. "We haven't seen you in awhile, Rosalie. What brings you here so suddenly?"

"Sit down, please," I said. "Both of you. I have something to say."

Mom sat down next to him on the couch, and they looked at me, waiting.

"Perry is in trouble," I said. "I brought him here, Dad, and he's upstairs in the bathroom getting cleaned up."

"Cleaned up?" he said. "What do you mean 'cleaned up'? What's he cleaning up?"

I took a deep breath. "Blood. He's cleaning blood off himself."

"Is he hurt?" Mom said. "Does he need a doctor?"

"He's not hurt," I said. "Maybe a few scratches, that's all. It's mostly not his blood he's cleaning off."

Dad suddenly narrowed his eyes and his voice lowered. "What do you mean? Did he get in a fight in a bar? What happened?"

I took another deep breath. "He killed someone. A woman name Margo Elden. She's the wife of a banker."

My mother put her hand to her mouth. "What? He killed a woman? Why? What happened? Was it an accident?"

"Rosalie, start at the beginning," Dad said. "What happened? How in God's name did he kill this woman? What was he doing?"

I just blurted it out. "He was having sex with her. Things took a bad turn. I do not want to go into details, but I guess he lost control somehow. I don't know much about it; he's not making much sense right now. All I know is he didn't intend for it to happen. It was an accident."

"An accident!" my father snorted. "The creep, what was he doing screwing around with her in the first place?" He stood up and started pacing the room. "I never liked that guy, Rosalie. I knew he

81

was bad news, but you wouldn't listen to me. You hang around with jerks like that, and look what happens!"

"Pete, he's right upstairs," Mom said.

"I don't give a shit where he is!" my father said. "The son of a bitch, doing something like that! They ought to fry his ass for that. Well, I won't have to worry about him being around you anymore, that's for sure. He's going away for a long time."

"No I'm not," Perry said.

We turned to see him on the stairs leading down into the den.

He was standing with a towel, wiping his hands, and there were bloodstains on the towel. His hair and clothes were a mess, and he looked ragged and wild-eyed. He came down the steps and stood facing us.

"I know you never liked me, Mr. Morley, but I swear I didn't mean to kill that woman. It just got out of hand, things started happening fast and she was pushing me so much. . . you have to believe me, I wouldn't do a thing like that. But regardless of what you think, I can not go to jail for this. I am not going, and that's all there is to it." His jaw was sticking out, and his fists were clenched, as if he thought he was going to have to fight his way out of the house.

For a moment I thought my Dad was going to go over and hit him, and my stomach tensed up as I waited for the collision. Instead, though, my father just stood there calmly and spoke in an even tone.

"You may not have meant to kill her, son, but you did. And whatever the circumstances, you have to own up to it. You can't run away, you have to face your crime. I don't know why you came here, but you have to go over there and pick up that phone," he pointed to a phone on the table next to the bookcase, "and you have to call the police right now and tell them what you did."

Perry looked at him and repeated, "No."

"What do you mean?" Dad said.

"I ain't calling nobody," Perry said, in a low voice. He threw the bloody hand towel on the floor. "I told you already, I'm not going to have my life taken away from me. I worked real hard to make something of myself, and I'm not throwing that away."

"You already threw it away when you killed that woman," my father said. His fists were clenched, and I braced myself to try and stop him from running at Perry. He didn't move, though. He just stood there, and I could hear him breathing heavily.

"That was just a bad thing that happened," Perry said. "I didn't have no control over that. It was that woman's fault, not mine. I ain't going to prison for something that she started." He turned to look at me. "Rosalie, you don't have to be part of this. I'm leaving now, and I'm taking the truck. I'm not asking you to do anything, you can just stay here and I'll go."

"No," I said. "Don't do that. Running isn't going to do any good. I don't know why I brought you here. I wasn't thinking straight. My Dad is right. We have to go to the police now. You have to follow the law."

He shook his head. "I'm not doing that. I'm not going anywhere but far away. I'm getting out of here now. You can call the cops later if you want. I'm not sticking around. Give me the keys to the truck."

"No," my father said. "Rosalie, don't do that."

My mother seemed scared, though. I could tell her body was trembling, and she was reaching a hand out to my father, as if to stop him from attacking Perry. I didn't want any more trouble, so I reached in the pocket of my jeans, pulled out the keys, and flipped them to Perry.

He caught them, said, "Goodbye, Rosalie. I'm sorry this happened," then he turned and bounded up the steps. In a moment I heard the front door open, and then the sound of the truck's ignition going on. Then there was the squeal of the tires as he raced down the long driveway.

My mother sat down on the couch and put her head in her hands. I went over and stood behind the couch and put my hand on her shoulder. It was all I could do.

"It's okay, Mom," I said. "Don't worry, everything will be all right."

"No it won't," my father said. "It won't be all right unless you call the police right now and tell them what happened. If you wait, you're going to be charged as an accessory. You have to report him."

"I know I do," I said. "I tried to do it in the hotel, but I lost my nerve. I guess I panicked, and that's why I came here. But Dad, isn't he going to be in bigger trouble now that he ran?"

"Yes," my father said. "He's in a lot of trouble now. He can't get away. They'll catch him, and it won't go well for him. Dammit,

Rosalie, I knew he was bad news years ago when you first started hanging around with him. I told you to stay away from him!"

"Pete, stop it," my mother said. "These things aren't rational. People fall in love with who they fall in love with. It's not some neat little thing you can control. Let her alone. She'll do the right thing." She turned and grabbed my hand. "Your father and I are going to go upstairs now. I know you'll do what's right. Come on, Pete."

Dad grumbled, but then he followed her upstairs. I was alone in the room, with a thousand conflicting thoughts crowding through me. I knew I should call the police, but I was worried for Perry, even though I knew I shouldn't be. After all, he'd just killed a woman not an hour before. Her body may have been discovered by now. I couldn't be a part of covering that up.

I reached for the phone and dialed 911.

CHAPTER THIRTEEN

I told you before that I do not like to be noticed, and that I always wish I could blend in with the background, so it was difficult for me to go through the next few months after October 17, 2007. I had to go through a lot of questioning by the police and lawyers and so forth, and even though I tried to be very precise with them about all the facts, they kept coming back to the same questions, as if they hadn't listened to my answers.

I think for a short time they thought I had something to do with Margo's death, and it took them a while to figure out I did not. I told them that I do not like breaking rules, and killing someone was breaking the biggest rule of all. I am glad that they finally understood what I was saying.

Of course, then they thought I knew where Perry was, and it took a while to convince them that I did not. "If I knew where he was I would tell you," I kept saying.

They finally believed me, but they told me to let them know if I ever heard from him. Which I would do, of course, but I did not know if I would ever hear from him. After all, it would be pretty stupid of him to get in touch with me now.

But just because I wasn't a suspect didn't mean that things were easy. Lambertville was a small town, and small town people talk. Rumors spread quickly, and people had all sorts of ideas about what was going on between Perry, Margo, and me. I heard things from friends, and I noticed how conversations would stop when I walked into my favorite coffee shop or deli, and I saw the way people looked at me. It was a problem, but I couldn't do anything about it, and I just kept my eyes down and went about my business. I thought about going to Margo's funeral, but I didn't want to cause a scene, or to take away from her funeral.

I saw Blake Elden, Margo's husband, only once. I was on my bike, waiting for a traffic light to change, when I felt like someone was looking at me. I turned to see two men standing at the light waiting to cross in front of me. One was Blake and the other man I did not know. It seemed like their conversation had just stopped before I turned, and they were both looking at me. I looked away quickly, but I could feel Blake's eyes on me for a long time as I waited for the light to change. I was glad when the light changed and I could pedal across the intersection.

I never thought Perry would get away. I always thought he'd be caught in a day or at most a week, holed up in some cheap motel, paralyzed with fear, unable to figure out what to do. As each day went by, I'd lie in my bed before falling asleep and wonder where he was, what he was doing. I kept measuring his progress in my head. Today he's probably in Michigan, I'd think. And the next day I'd be certain he was west of Chicago, or maybe as far as Nebraska. I had a big map of the United States on the wall in my bedroom, and I'd look at it and wonder where Perry was on the map.

The days turned into weeks, and I marked them off on a calendar in my kitchen. I had a lot of questions, like what was Perry doing for money? Where was he living? Did he change his appearance? I did not think he would use his credit cards, because he knew the charges could be traced, and besides, I was still doing the books and the banking for the business and I would have known about any charges. No, the charges stopped, and I figured Perry just threw the cards away. He was always the secretive type, and I figured he had a stash of money somewhere that he'd taken with him.

But no matter how much cash he had, it wouldn't last forever. At some point he'd have to get a job, and that would require a Social Security number, a residence, all that stuff. There was a structure to the world, like a huge grid, it seemed to me, and you had to fit in there somewhere. Everybody did. If you wanted to exist in this world, you had to find your place and fit in. Some people like me and Perry had a hard time finding our spot, and that was the frustrating part. It was like the world was a huge long train that stopped at a station, and we got on and looked for a seat in the first car, but it was full. Then we walked down the aisle and went through the door to the second car, but that one was full also. So, we kept going on and on, through hundreds, thousands of train cars, but in every one the seats were taken by people, everybody dressed the same and looking exactly the same, but very different from us. So, we just keep walking through the cars as the train lurches along and the people all look at us as we walk past, and all we want to do is find a place to sit down.

Sometimes I thought that maybe Perry finally found his place to sit down, and that he was happy now. He was good with his hands, he could do carpentry and plumbing and all sorts of things, and maybe he was working as a handyman in some little town, doing odd jobs and getting paid in cash. He might have had some peace, but then again nobody would know who he was, which would bother him, because he wanted so much to be known, to be put on a pedestal.

Perry wanted success, it was the only thing he really cared about, and I thought it must be killing him if he had to pretend to be someone else. He wanted the world to know that Perry Lukens had made something of himself, had become a somebody. He would not like being a nobody again, a zero, in his eyes. An assumed identity would not sit well with him.

The other question in my mind was if I'd ever see him again. I was still shocked at what he'd done, and I did not like that he'd run away, but in spite of all his flaws I still cared for him. It was strange, I know, because I never told him I loved him, and he never told me he loved me, either. I don't use words like "love" very easily. It's one of those words that's a puzzle to me. I see lots of people who are supposed to be in love but they don't talk that way to each other, or they don't act that way. I do not use that word because it's uncomfortable for me to say it, but with Perry I tried to express it in different ways. I knew he was an imperfect, flawed person, but so was I. I thought we somehow fit together well, each one making up for the other's defects in some way.

Sometimes my parents would ask me if I'd heard from Perry. I think they were worried I'd say yes, but I always said no. "Are you kidding?" I'd say to my father. "He's long gone. I'll never hear from him again," but I don't think my parents completely believed me.

Another reason why it was hard to get Perry out of my mind was that I was still going to the office every day and dealing with the mess he left behind. It was a disaster, like trying to put your life back together after a tornado. Perry's company was falling apart in front of my eyes. The economy had soured, it was the middle of the real estate crisis and mortgages had dried up, and contractors were going bankrupt all over the State. There was no work to be had, and even if there was, I don't think anyone would have hired a company that used to belong to a suspected murderer.

But the creditors didn't stop calling just because Perry had killed someone. Blake Elden stopped coming by the way he used to, and I was glad for that. However, he had an assistant, an annoying person named Ellen, who kept calling, and her voice on the phone was like fingernails on a blackboard. She was shouting all the time about the loans, and after a while I stopped answering her phone calls.

It was just me by myself in the office, like the last woman on a sinking ship, and I guess the bank finally took pity on me. They recommended a bankruptcy lawyer, a man named Jerry McAndrews, and I was glad for his help. He was a stubby, no-nonsense man with bushy red hair and a habit of saying the truth.

I got along fine with him.

Jerry didn't believe in using a lot of words. "This company is screwed," he said one day. "You can try to sell it, but if anybody's stupid enough to buy a home building and remodeling company in this economy, they'll give you five cents on the dollar. My advice is to lay everybody off, declare bankruptcy, and try to get out of this thing with your sanity."

I agreed. It was March 21, 2008, and all I wanted at that point was to walk out of that office, lock the door, and never come back. The bank was foreclosing on any property Perry owned, and that was fine with me. Jerry said there would be lawsuits, and they would drag on for years, but it was better to get out now before the company got further in debt.

On December 10, 2008 Jerry said it was time to close the office, and he said he'd sell off all the furniture and office equipment. "I'll give you a paycheck till Christmas," he said. "I hate doing this around the holidays, but there's no choice. We have to end this."

I walked outside at 4:00 PM and I went down to the river to look at it. It was slate gray, the same shade as the sky, and there was a cold wind blowing across it. The trees stretched their bare arms, as if pointing at some horror that was coming. There were Christmas lights blinking on, and somewhere I could hear a Christmas song playing. It seemed bizarre, the happy song playing on such a bleak afternoon in winter.

I thought of Perry, and I wondered what he was doing right now. Was he cold? Hungry? Hurt in any way? He'd worked so hard to build his little empire, and now it was all destroyed. It was funny how things could fall apart like that. The whole thing made me think even more that I should stay away from people. They were so unpredictable, so strange, and you never knew how they could damage you if you got involved with them. People were really good at hurting other people. Killing them, even. The safer thing was to stick with the things I liked: music, art, computers.

"Where are you, Perry?" I said, softly. "Where did you go? I hope your demons aren't too bad today. I don't think I can wish you peace, but I hope you aren't suffering too much." It had been thirteen months and twenty one days since the murder. I knew Perry had to be punished, but it was still hard to get used to that idea. There were so many loose ends, so many things left undecided between us.

"It's a hard time of year, isn't it?" said a voice behind me, and I turned to see Jack Caldwell, my grandma Rosie's widowed husband, standing there in his leather jacket with the collar turned up, a cigarette in his mouth.

CHAPTER FOURTEEN

"Jack?" I said. "You got old." Things like that always pop out of my mouth. Some people get mad at me when I talk like that, but Jack did not.

He laughed. "I haven't seen enough of you, Rosalie. I miss the way you just say whatever's on your mind."

"It has been a while since I've seen you," I said. "You have white hair now."

It had been eight years since Rosie's death, and it looked like they'd been hard ones for Jack.

He laughed. "Yeah, I'm an old guy now, Rosalie. I still ride my motorcycle, though, and I smoke cigarettes. I do all the stupid things I did when I was 25. I'm not ready for the old age home yet!"

"No," I said. "You look like you aren't."

"How are you, though?" he said, blowing cigarette smoke into the frigid air. "I was just thinking that Christmas is not such a good time for your family. Besides your boyfriend's incident last year, and Rosie dying on New Year's Eve, there have been other things. Rosie told me when she was a little girl she remembered her father was sent to prison just before Christmas in the 1940s. And further back than that, her grandfather, your great-grandfather, left his wife on New Year's Day in 1900. He abandoned her with three small children, one of whom was Rosie's father. It's a cursed time of year for you folks."

"I guess it is," I said. "It's funny, isn't it? We do things backward in this family. This is supposed to be a happy time, but not for us."

He laughed. "Yes, your family does things differently." He came over and gave me a hug. I don't normally like hugs, but he seemed so frail I let him do it. I could feel his thin arms underneath the jacket. "Now, really, how are you doing?" he said, pulling back to look at me.

"I'm okay," I said. "I'm tired of this guessing game, though. I keep wondering where Perry is, if he's alive, what he's doing, that kind of thing. I got used to being with him, and I miss that. My life is so upside down now. I'm at a crossroads. I'm thinking of going to school for computer programming. Today was my last day at the office. They're shutting it down, selling everything. Pretty soon there won't be anything left of Perry."

"He's probably far away," Jack said.

"Probably," I said. "I have to stop thinking about him. I have to move on."

"You'll see him again, I believe," Jack said.

"Ha! I doubt that," I said, shivering. "He's probably dead by now. Or, he's living in some foreign country. Although I never thought he'd survive if he lived somewhere else. He'd stand out like a sore thumb if he was living in some village in Mexico. He can't speak any languages, and he's not very flexible. He stands out, like I do. No, if they haven't caught him, he's probably dead."

"Have you had any dreams about him?" Jack said.

"No, I have not."

"Well, don't be surprised if you do. And pay attention to them, Rosalie. They might tell you something."

I laughed. "Jack Caldwell, you surprise me. I thought you were all about rational things, not dreams. I thought you were one of these numbers guys who only believe in ones and zeroes. Aren't you all about technology? I did not think someone like you would believe in messages in dreams. That's a surprise."

He smiled. "There are lots of things about me you probably don't know. But I'm getting cold standing here -- the only concession I make to age these days is that I don't like being cold. Why don't we go back to my place and have a cup of coffee? It's getting too frigid out here."

So I went back with him over the bridge to his apartment upstairs from Rosie's old restaurant. He had sold the restaurant several years before, and the new owner had kept it pretty much the same. One of the conditions of the sale was that Jack could live rent-free upstairs in the apartment forever, because he didn't want to move. He enjoyed hearing the noise from the restaurant, he said. It made him feel less alone.

The restaurant was decked out in Christmas decorations with a tree in one corner and vintage Santa Claus posters everywhere, and we went up the stairs to Jack's apartment. I hadn't been inside it in a long time, and I noticed right away that he'd kept it virtually the same as it was when Rosie was alive. The big blue overstuffed easy chair with the flower pattern, the lemon yellow sofa, the posters on the wall from the big band era, the doo-wop albums next to a vintage record player in the living room. It was an odd juxtaposition with the three computers with huge screens set up on a large desk just off the kitchen. The glowing screens lent an eerie quality to that corner of the apartment.

"How about a coffee?" Jack said. "I have some good Colombian I can make."

"Sure," I said, settling in to the couch. "I remember your coffee. It's the best."

Jack busied himself in the kitchen and I sat there awash with memories, remembering the last time Rosie had us over, on Christmas Eve in 1999. It was when Jack proposed to her in front of the whole family, and she had cried with joy and said yes. We had no idea she would be dead in a week.

Jack came back with two steaming mugs of coffee, and I took a sip of mine, letting the rich, dark flavor sink down inside me.

"This is good stuff," I said. "I would be such a coffee addict if I could get this every day. It's better than anything I've had in a Starbucks."

"I know," Jack said, taking a sip from his mug. "I live on this stuff. I get some of my best ideas when I'm drinking it. If I ever run out, the quality of my work suffers."

"You still look busy, judging from the computer setup over there," I said, pointing to the huge screens. "I'm amazed at you, Jack. You're still ahead of the curve, even at your age."

"I have to be," he said. "I turned 80 last year. There aren't many companies who'd hire an 80-year-old futurist unless he could impress the pants off them with his knowledge. If I don't know more than some 20-year-old geek in his parents' basement, I've failed. But I have to be able to give them more than that. I need to go beyond geek knowledge to another dimension. I have to use my creativity, my subconscious, my emotions, anything I can use to come up with my predictions, my long range thinking. It's way more than computer stuff, Rosalie. It's like Geek ESP."

"You've lost me," I said. "What's that?"

"It's a way of looking at reality," he said, sipping from his mug. "It's recognizing that this world is a lot more complex than just being reduced to a binary formula. I think a lot of people are making a mistake these days, assuming that we can figure everything out with the aid of our gadgets. It's like we think eventually there will be a computer or a program that will give us all the answers to the existential questions we have at 3 in the morning. That ain't gonna happen. Computers only go so far."

"You sound like an old man," I said. "Like somebody who wishes we did not use computers so much. Well, I like computers. I grew up with them, and I like how they organize things. I think they can help us figure things out. You know, I am 28, Jack. I need to figure out what I'm doing with my life. I think computers are the field to go into. I mean, some of the stuff I read about what's coming -- it's amazing."

He looked over at the screens. "They are mind blowing, for sure," he said. "And they're going to make a lot of changes in our lives. You will live to see some astonishing things, Rosalie. It's just, technology will always have this aura of promise, of getting it all right, giving us all the answers with just one more new program, one more update, one more new application or one more new gadget. We're forever chasing a dream that's dimly visible in the screen, but we never quite catch it. To be truly transformative, you have to use the other tools at your disposal."

"Like what?" I said.

"Like your subconscious," he said, touching his heart. "The deep, dark, magical place where dreams, poetry and religion come from. That's part of our humanity. The machines will never be able to give us those answers. We have to find them ourselves, from deep within."

"I don't think I understand you," I said. "How can dreams give any answers? I mean, there are times when I've gotten lottery ticket numbers from a dream, but mostly dreams are just confusing."

He sat up in his chair. "What did you say about lottery tickets?"

I laughed. "Oh, twice I dreamed winning lottery ticket numbers. Those were strange dreams, I have to admit. Perry thought I was psychic or something, and he kept asking me to dream some more numbers, because he won enough on one of the tickets to start his business. It never happened again, though. Just some weird, unexplainable thing."

"That's an amazing ability you have," he said. "It doesn't surprise me, though, because your grandmother Rosie had it. She definitely was tuned into the subconscious. She heard voices and saw visions all the time. She didn't pay attention to it for years, but later in life she treated it with more respect. I think all of the women in your family have the gift."

I shook my head. "It didn't do her any good, though, did it? She didn't get a vision about when she was going to die, Jack. If she did, she wouldn't have tried to cross the street at that exact moment on New Years' Eve. I think that stuff is a bunch of horse manure."

"Well, what about your lottery dreams?"

I paused. "Sure, they were different, not ordinary dreams. I have no explanation, except that they were a couple of random dreams that happened to turn out. I sure don't think they were sent to me by someone from another dimension. Really, Jack, I'm surprised at you. For a guy who's spent his whole life in technology and science, you're talking like a hippie girl from the 1960s."

He smiled. "Yeah, I guess I am. Well, I've always kept an open mind about that stuff. You know, my view of reality is a lot different than the average person's. I lived in California in the late 1950s, and I participated in some experiments at Stanford University where they gave us LSD. You probably didn't know that, did you?"

"No, I did not," I said.

"Well, it's true. I dropped acid under controlled conditions. Bunch of guys in white lab coats in a room measuring our heart rate, blood pressure, that sort of thing. They were trying to find out if they could use this new drug for CIA interrogations. They thought it might work as a truth serum, I guess. I got paid a few bucks for it, which came in handy since I was a poor graduate student."

"What happened?"

"I saw beneath the surface of reality. We're all connected, Rosalie. Time and space are illusions. It's all one big tapestry, one big soup with everything, past, present and future in it. I know it sounds crazy, but that's what I perceived. The universe is one big beating heart. There are a billion stories out there, a billion trillion souls all connected on a fundamental level. The trouble is that we don't recognize it, and we are blinded by our greedy egos that want their own little empires. We turn away from real beauty every day, we get distracted by so many things that have no value, that are just shiny, pretty things that keep us from the truth."

I laughed. "You sound like you belong back in the 1960s, Jack. Like you should be wearing a long robe and sandals, and smoking weed. I thought we were past all that hippy dippy stuff. The world isn't like that; at least I don't think so. It's hard for people to fit together. A big beating heart? Hearts are messy things, and they cause problems."

Jack sighed. "I feel bad for your generation, if that's how you see the world. We've failed you, it seems. Sure, hearts are messy, and they can be broken, but they also are what makes us human. They connect us in so many ways."

"I read about the 1960s in school," I said. "That's when all the hippies started communes, right? They thought everything should be about free love and sharing. That didn't work very well, did it? People are too nasty to live together like that."

"That's the narrative the world wants you to believe," Jack said. "It's not that way at all. If you just let yourself go, you'll find out. You have a gift, Rosalie, and you should use it to tap into the love at the root of all things. You should. Wait, I want to give you something." He got up and went down the hall to another room. While he was gone I looked at the screen savers on his computer, which were all images of the Beatles from the Flower Power era.

He came back and sat down across from me and handed me something. It was a rosary, with simple wooden beads connected with a metal chain.

"What is this?" I said.

"It's your grandmother's rosary," he said. "And she got it from her grandmother, Rose. The one who came over from Ireland. I'm pretty sure she got it from her own mother back in Ireland. The story I heard is that it was a gift they gave to her when she left her town to come to America. It's very old. I'm giving it to you."

"Thanks, Jack," I said. "But I don't really practice any religion. I'm not a believer, you know." I handed it back. "I'd rather not."

He put his hands up. "No, please take it. I want you to have it. You don't have to use it, Rosalie. Just keep it with you. It's a connection with your Irish roots."

I took the rosary and stuffed it in my pocket. It was a strange conversation with Jack, and I didn't know what to make of it. He talked for hours about how he was afraid we were all making too many compromises with technology, bending ourselves to fit into a pattern that wasn't natural or human. We needed to get in touch with our humanity, he kept saying.

Finally, I just said, "Jack, you still sound like an old hippie to me. I don't understand half of what you're saying. Maybe that LSD changed your brain chemistry all those years ago. I don't want to get in touch with humanity, because people are too crazy and stupid and unpredictable. I want to deal in certainties, in simple answers, and in formulas. After the year I just had, I want predictability. I want to learn everything there is to know about computers, and I want you to teach me."

Jack smiled. "Okay, Rosalie. If that's what you want, I'll help you."

CHAPTER FIFTEEN

I started spending a lot of time at Jack's apartment, and I supplemented that with classes I took at a local college. I was hungry to learn all I could, and I made progress fast. Within six months I was helping Jack with his consulting business, and in the space of a year I was hiring myself out to local businesses (based on Jack's recommendations of me) to help set up computer networks for them. The pay was good, and I was able to afford a better apartment, better clothes, and better furniture. I even bought a pet, a rabbit I named Charly. He was white with floppy ears, and I kept him in a cage, but I let him roam around the apartment when I was home.

Computer consulting was a good gig for me. Clients viewed me as a geek and they didn't expect a lot chitchat from me in person, so they pretty much left me alone in a back office to work on their systems. In fact, the less I talked to them, the smarter they thought I was. When I developed a sideline in building Websites it was even better -- I hardly ever had to meet with the clients. I got work through Websites that had freelance job postings, and I just did my work, uploaded it, and got paid.

As I got busier and made more money I did not have as much time for Jack. I regret it now, but I got caught up in my life and did not pay attention to the fact that he was getting older and more frail. He still kept up his pace, but things took him longer now, and I didn't catch on.

By December of 2010 he was slowing down considerably. It made sense -- he was 83 years old. I had just turned 30 and I was busier than ever. I had money in the bank, and I decided to buy Jack an expensive Christmas present. It was a fancy pen and pencil set, ordered from a London company that was famous for them. I got it because Jack was always complaining that people never wrote letters anymore.

I waited till 7:00 on Christmas Eve, and then I went to his apartment, which was still above Rosie's old restaurant. The door was locked, but I had a key, because Jack still traveled a lot and he wanted me to be able to come in whenever I wanted. I knew he wouldn't be out of town on Christmas Eve, though. I unlocked the door and went inside, and there was the familiar glare of his computer screens, but he was nowhere to be found.

"Jack?" I said. Suddenly, my skin started tingling, and the hairs on the back of my neck stood up. It was too quiet, and I knew something was wrong. There was no one in the kitchen, although there was a kettle on a lit burner on the stove. It was not boiling, which meant it hadn't been there long.

I went into the bedroom, and Jack was lying on his side on the floor next to the bed, as if he'd tried to get out of bed and collapsed. His cell phone was in his hand. His mouth was open and his eyes were staring at nothing.

I knelt down and felt his wrist, but there was no pulse. He was dead. I sat next to him on the floor and cradled his head in my arms.

"Why did you leave, Jack?" I said. "Why?"

I don't know why I always have to be the one to find dead bodies. It's like people wait till they know I'll be around before they die. Me, the person who least knows how to handle these things.

I couldn't believe this good, kind man was gone. I had known him all my life and he'd always been a guide and beacon to me, someone I could talk to about anything. I regretted losing touch with him for so long. He had a wide, deep knowledge but he was never arrogant about it. He always treated you like you had some knowledge of your own to share with him, even though he seemed to know something about almost everything, and I seriously wondered when I'd ever told him anything he didn't already know.

Now he was gone.

At the funeral, which was 10:00 AM on January 3, 2011, I sat in the church with my parents and some other friends of the family, and I kept wishing I was a hawk and I could fly away, over the river. I didn't know how I'd survive without Jack to talk to. I was 30 years old and already I'd seen death up close three times. It did not make any sense to me.

I reached in my pocket at the funeral and felt the rosary, long forgotten in the inside pocket of a winter jacket. I mumbled the words to the Hail Mary under my breath and felt comforted, though I didn't know how or why. I wrote a eulogy for Jack, and I told my parents I was going to give it. I had never spoken in front of a group of people before, and I did not know how I was going to pull it off.

I decided it was something I should do for Jack, though. It was hard to stand up there and talk about what he meant to me, but I managed to get through it without having a heart attack, although I had to stop several times to catch my breath.

There was a luncheon at a restaurant after Jack's funeral, and I met people who'd worked with Jack or known him for many years. People came from all over the country, some of them his friends from the days in California in the 1950s through the 1970s. There were people there from all walks of life, everyone from CEOs of tech companies, to tai chi masters, to cab drivers he'd stayed in touch with.

I milled around at the luncheon, wondering what to do with myself, and I finally decided to just eat some food and get out of there. I was waiting in line at a buffet table when someone tapped me on the shoulder. I turned and I was at eye level with the chest of a very large man. He was tall and red-haired with bushy red eyebrows and broad shoulders, and eyes the color of the sky. He looked kind of outdoorsy, with a sunburned face and huge, weathered hands.

"That was a beautiful eulogy," he said. "Jack would be proud of you."

"Thank you," I said. "I never did one of those before."

"You know, I didn't picture you as so petite."

"You didn't picture me?" I said. "How do you know about me?"

"Jack talked about you all the time," he said. "He always said good things about you."

"Well, who are you?" I asked.

"The name's Ryan Frazier," he said, bowing slightly. "At your service. Do you mind if I sit at your table? I don't know many people here, and it would be more fun to talk to you than some of the geeks here."

I said yes, so we got our food and went over to a nearby table and sat down. It was a big round table and there were ten other people sitting at it. We introduced ourselves, but then Ryan and I had our own private conversation.

"So how did you know Jack?" I asked when we sat down.

"Well, I teach the history and psychology of computers," he said. "I took a seminar in grad school that Jack taught, 20 years ago. I found him the most fascinating person I'd ever met in the field, and I made it my business to stay in touch with him. He had such a breadth of knowledge, such an appreciation for so many things. He was a pleasure to talk to. I called him regularly, and we got together whenever he came out to the West Coast. It's a shame, really, because I just moved out here a month ago, and I was looking forward to seeing him more. I never thought I had enough time with him."

"That's life," I said. "One thing I've learned is you can't predict when somebody is going to leave you. It happens all the time. It sucks, really."

"It makes you appreciate every day," Ryan said.

"No, what it means to me is you shouldn't get involved with people," I said. "All they do is leave."

He looked at me and smiled. "That's a funny idea from a friend of Jack Caldwell's. He was all about human relationships. I remember him saying we were all getting too wrapped up in technology, and forgetting about our human relationships," he said, buttering a roll and taking a bite of it. "He believed human relationships need nurturing and we're not taking the time for that."

"Can you blame anyone for that?" I said. "Human

relationships are complicated. They're unpredictable, random and volatile. No wonder people prefer to spend time on their computers. They're safer, easier to control."

"That's quite a harsh view of things," he offered. "I don't think it's that bad. At least, people didn't think that way for millions of years. It's only been recently that people are shying away from human contact in favor of machines. Sure, computers are more predictable, and you don't have to deal with messy emotions. And yes, they don't leave you. But it's going to be a sterile, heartless world if everyone thinks like you do."

"You're one to talk," I said. "You make your living teaching about technology, don't you?"

"Yes I do," he said. "I have a doctorate in computer engineering. But I have other degrees -- psychology, history -- you can't put me in a box."

"Well, I don't understand why you think it's so bad being in the computer field," I said. "Computers have made the world a better place, haven't they? I think we need to spend more time developing them, more time in front of the screens, not less. That's where the real progress will come in this world. We're eliminating diseases, and before long I think we'll get rid of things like war, poverty, crime. Computers and technology are making the world better. I don't see what's not to like."

"See, that's what I'm talking about," he said. "So many people think technology will set us free, make us better people. I think we're rushing headlong into a new world without paying attention to the dangers. I mean, there are people talking seriously about downloading their consciousness into machines. What kind of a world would that be? These machines are supposed to be our tools, not the other way around."

"I think you're crazy," I said. "You sound like you're reading from some cheap sci-fi novel about robots taking over. It's crap. Besides, whatever machines can do for us is good, if they can eliminate some of the flaws in human nature. Imagine all the good that will come when the world isn't ruled by emotion anymore."

His face reddened, and his voice rose. "Didn't you learn anything from Jack?" he said. "The last twenty years of his life he was warning against that very idea. He said it was dangerous, and we shouldn't be seduced by the promise of perfect, rational lives without the messiness of emotions. That's what we think we'll get with computers, but it's a false view. We're giving up part of our humanity if we go in that direction. My God, woman," he thundered, slapping his hand on the table, "what's wrong with you?"

I felt my own face reddening. "There's nothing wrong with me at all. You're the one who's wrong! I never agreed with all that stuff Jack talked about, and I told him so. He was just getting old and soft, I think. I mean, computers have worked wonders for us, and anybody who thinks it's wrong to become more like them is crazy. They represent the best human achievement ever, and I don't see any negatives about them."

By this time the other people at our table had gotten very silent, and as my voice rose an octave at the end of the sentence, it hung there in the air like a ringing bell. I don't like people staring at me, and I quickly cleared my throat and said, "Excuse me, I need to go to the restroom."

Inside the restroom I was shaking, and it took me a while to calm down. Come on, Rosalie, I said to myself. Don't cause a scene at Jack's funeral. This guy isn't worth it. I did a deep breathing exercise, patted my face with a wet paper towel, and then combed my hair and re-applied my makeup. When I was finally calm, I went out to the the dining room again and purposely avoided the table. I mingled with the other guests, and spent a long time looking at old pictures of Jack that my brother had put together on a poster board. Many of them had my grandmother Rosie in them, and it brought back memories, like the night that she died.

I wondered if I would ever find a relationship like Rosie and Jack had. I was 30, and there was nothing on the horizon. It's never easy for me to form relationships with anyone, let alone people I might want to spend my life with. Maybe I'd be one of those people who go through life and never find that one special person. Well, it was one more reason to bury myself in my work, it seemed. At least work didn't let you down.

"He had a brilliant smile, especially when he was around your grandmother," a voice said. I turned to see Ryan Frazier standing next to me, looking at the poster.

"Yes," I said.

"I'm sorry about what happened," he said. "I didn't mean for that discussion to turn into an argument."

"Yeah well it did," I said. "Look, I don't see where we have anything in common. I think we should just stop talking now."

"I feel bad," he said. "I hate leaving things like this. I'm really not such a terrible guy. I'd love to take you out for coffee and show you a different side of me."

"I don't see the point in that," I said. "I've already determined that we don't get along, so why should we continue this?"

"Please?" he said. "I just think it would be great to restart this. Besides, I'm new here. I really don't know many people besides you. Maybe you could tell me about the area. Really. I don't bite. I promise."

I shrugged. "Okay, if you want to. But I don't know how much I can tell you. I kind of stick to myself. I don't have friends, really. Not much of a social life. I live alone, with my pet rabbit. I'm probably not the best person--"

"No, you'll be fine," he said. "Just fine. How about tomorrow? Are you available in the morning around 11?"

I hesitated, wondering if I should say yes. It seemed like maybe it was time to start a new pattern, though. You can't just keep doing the same thing all the time, no matter how comfortable it is.

"Sure," I said. "I rent office space at the Benton building, on State and Main, just across the bridge in Lambertville. I'm on the second floor, number 205. Come by at 11."

CHAPTER SIXTEEN

The next day when Julie, the girl who works at the front desk, told me there was a large man with red hair waiting to see me, I had completely forgotten about Ryan Frazier. I was immersed in designing a Website for a client, a garden center in Bucks County, and when I get involved in something I forget about everything else around me. Sometimes it seems to take me a few seconds to remember who I am and where I am.

Anyway, I was annoyed that Ryan had interrupted me, but I stopped work and put on my jacket and met him, and he was wearing brown shoes with tan pants and I didn't smile at him, I just said, "Come on," and led him out the door and down the street to The Benton Cafe where I sometimes go for coffee.

I picked my same table, which is near the street so I can count the birds that fly by. Counting things helps me and I like to do it. I was going to get my own coffee but Ryan said he would get coffee for both of us, so I told him what I wanted which was a medium latte with just a splash of half and half and one packet of sugar in it. When he brought it back and put it down I took a sip and suddenly didn't know what to say, so I stared outside.

"Well, it's a delightful day, isn't it?" he said. "Gorgeous blue sky, and the air crisp and cold. You know, I'm not used to this. In California we don't get this kind of cold. Winter is pretty intense here, but I like it. It has a bracing effect, don't you think?

"I guess so," I said. I didn't know what to say. It felt weird to see him out of the context of the funeral. I had to get used to it.

There was a silence, so I said, "Do you know the arctic tern, which weighs only four ounces, makes the longest annual migration of any bird in the world? Each year they travel 44,000 miles from Greenland to Antarctica and back again. Did you know that?"

"I didn't know that," he said.

"I love birds," I said. "I love reading about them and imagining what it would be like to be a bird. I love thinking about their migrations. I love that they leave one part of the world and make this perilous journey to another part, and then fly back, and they do it all over again the next year. It's fascinating to me. I would like to be a bird."

"Yes, they are fascinating creatures," he said. "I went to see the swallows of Capistrano when I lived in California. It gave me such a lift to see them flying back from their journey."

"I think birds are really dinosaurs that have evolved," I said. "Scientists are not agreed on that, but I think it's true. They became smaller and more mobile, and they were better able to survive than the big, clumsy creatures they were millions of years ago. That's my opinion, anyway. So, why are you here?"

"I love the way your mind operates," he said, with a laugh. "It makes so many interesting connections. I guess the subject of bird migration made you think of me moving here?"

"I don't know," I said. "My brain just does what it does. I don't question it so much."

"Well, to answer your question, I came here because I wanted a change. I lived in California for many years, and I thought I'd like to see what the East is like. I found a teaching job here, and I just moved. I didn't plan it much. I threw out or sold most of my stuff, because I wanted to start fresh. I'm sad that Jack died, because I was looking forward to spending more time with him, but that's life."

"I don't want to talk about Jack," I said.

"I understand," he said. "Well, as I was saying, I wanted to start fresh."

"Are you married?" I said.

"No," he said. "I am not. I used to be, many years ago. It was a youthful mistake, I guess. We weren't suited for each other. It ended painfully, but that's in the past."

"I don't like the past," I said. "I would rather live in the present. That's why I like birds. They live in the present. All they care about is the present. If something bad happens, they don't worry about it, they just fly away."

"That might work for birds, but not for people," he said. "People can't avoid the past. It's always with them. They can't fly away from it, unfortunately."

"I like to know dates," I said. "I do like that. I have pictures in my mind for every date. The past is just a progression of pictures to me."

"But we can learn from the past," Ryan Frazier said. "Don't you think? It has lessons to teach us."

"I don't know," I said. "Maybe. I just like to fix all the pictures in their proper order. I don't think about putting it all together."

He shook his head. "My, my, Rosalie, you certainly have a different perspective on things. But how about your past? Tell me about yourself. Have you lived here all your life?"

"No. When I was little we lived in the city. We moved here when I was in high school, on June 5, 1994, because the schools were better and my parents wanted to get out of the city. I like it better here because there are more birds than in the city. My grandmother died ten years ago on New Year's Eve. I had a boyfriend named Perry, who ran a construction business. I dreamed a lottery number than won him lots of money and he started his business. He did well, but then the economy went bad and his business went bad. He killed a woman in a hotel in Stockton, New Jersey."

He sucked in his breath. "Killed a woman? How did that happen? Was it an accident?"

"He strangled her," I said. "Strangulation is not an accident. If you put your hands around someone's neck in the area of the carotid arteries, larynx, or trachea, and squeeze hard for a minimum of two minutes you will block the flow of oxygen to their brain and they will die."

"I understand the physiology of it," he said. "But why? What happened to make him kill her?"

"He was doing something dirty with her. That is all I will say."

There was a pause. "I see," Ryan said. "I'm sorry."

"You don't need to be sorry. You had nothing to do with it."

"I know that. It's just an expression."

"It's a stupid expression. I never know why people use it."

"I suppose you're right," Ryan said. "When did all this happen?"

"Five years, three months, and ten days ago."

"What happened to your boyfriend? Is he in prison?"

"He ran away. They never caught him."

"I see," Ryan said. "That must have been a traumatic time for you."

"It was worse for him. He's the one who killed someone."

"I hope you don't mind me asking," he said. "But do you have anyone you're seeing now?"

"Seeing?" I said. "I don't know what you mean."

He cleared his throat. "I just mean, you know, are you in a relationship with anyone? Dating?"

"I keep to myself," I said. "Perry was the only boyfriend I've had." I pushed my chair back and stood up. "I have to go back to work. I have an important project I'm working on. Thank you for the coffee."

"You're welcome," he said.

He reached across the table and touched my arm, but I pulled my arm away fast.

"What are you doing?" I said. "I don't like people touching me."

"Oh, I'm sorry," he said. "I just wanted to ask, uh, would you like to go out? I would love to take you out somewhere. Would that be possible? You know, I have a great idea. I'm supposed to meet someone in Greenton tomorrow night. I have this hobby; I play the organ for silent movies. I'm a big silent film buff, I belong to several film societies, and I learned how to do the accompaniment for the movies. Anyway, I met someone at a silent film conference in California last year, and he told me he was part of a group that was restoring an old theater in a place called Greenton, about an hour north of here. It's run by a film society, and they play silent films regularly. I kept in touch with this guy, and when I moved out here I contacted him about playing the organ. I have a tryout tomorrow, where I'm going to play along with a film and if they like me they'll use my services for their next film festival. I'd love if you'd come along."

"I don't know anything about silent films," I said.

"Well, you can learn," he said. "They're fascinating, believe me. I'm sure you could learn a great deal from them. And you'll enjoy them immensely."

"I don't know," I said.

"Why not?" he said. "The weather is supposed to be sunny tomorrow. It could be a great day to take a drive along the river. I could pick you up at 5 and we'd be there by 6:00. I'd really love it."

"I have to get back to work," I said. "I will go with you tomorrow. Goodbye." And I left. I didn't know why I said yes to him, but it was done, so I had to accept it.

115

I left the coffee shop and took the long route back to the office, so I could walk along the river and look for my hawk. I had found a big hawk that roosted in the top branches of a tall oak tree near the river, and I liked to see him. Sometimes he'd be riding the heat thermals that came off the river, and I liked to see how he just glided along up there so free and easy. I found him right away, just floating along on those air currents, and I watched him for a few minutes, wondering what it would be like to be up there, just coasting along looking down at the water and the houses and the cars passing by over the bridge.

When I got back to the office it was lunchtime and a lot of people had left the building. I never locked the door to my office, because it was a safe town that I lived in, so I just walked in and took my jacket off and hung it up. When I turned around, though, something caught my eye.

It was a piece of paper that was taped to my computer screen. It was yellow lined paper, like one of those legal pads, and it had words on it that were stuck on, like those alphabet letters you can buy at Staples that they make for kids to stick on their art projects. The letters were red and they spelled out: "YOU ARE EVIL AND YOU WILL BE PUNISHED."

I sat down and tore the paper off the screen and looked at it for a long time. I didn't know if someone was playing a joke, but it wasn't funny to me.

CHAPTER SEVENTEEN

I thought it was odd that somebody would leave a note like that taped to my computer. I couldn't figure out why. I thought about it for awhile, then I took the note and folded it carefully and put it in my desk drawer. I went back to my work, but it was hard to concentrate. Sometimes I get thoughts that won't go away, they keep hanging around my brain, and the thought about the note just wouldn't go away. It was hard to concentrate on my work for the rest of the afternoon, and I finally turned my computer off at 5:00 and decided I would go home and try to stop thinking about it.

When I left the office I locked the door. It was something I didn't usually do, but this time I thought I would do it. I went outside and walked down to the river to look at my hawk, and I saw him in the top branches of his tree. He just perched there motionless, turning his head with quick little movements, and you'd probably never notice him if you didn't know to look for him like I did. I liked that he was sitting up there looking over his world, scanning the boundaries of it and making sure everything was all right. I felt like I was part of his domain, and he was watching over me too.

I stopped at a deli to get a pita sandwich for my dinner, and I talked to Angie, the girl who works there. We like to talk about music, all kinds of different music, and she told me she found some YouTube videos with The Magnificent Men in them. They were a singing group from York, PA that was around in the 1960s and they had some regional hits but they never made it big. They had a big, soulful sound that I loved, and although they were all white, they sounded black. They were actually booked at black theaters like the Apollo, and the audiences loved them. I love talking about obscure groups like that with Angie. Now I couldn't wait to get home so I could look up those YouTube videos of The Magnificent Men. I said goodbye to her and walked the four blocks to my apartment building.

I let myself in the front door and went up the 24 steps to the second floor, then down the hallway past Apartment 201 and 202, to my apartment, 203. I put my key in the lock and opened the door, and I went in and right away I knew something was different. I keep everything in its place, you see, and I could tell that something was out of place. I looked at the chairs and the couch and the lamps and the table and everything seemed normal, but I still knew something was different.

I went in the kitchen and then I saw it. On the counter on top of the wooden cutting board, was my rabbit Charly, and there was a knife sticking in him. He was dead, and there was blood everywhere, and I screamed. I dropped my sandwich and ran out, down the steps and out on to the street.

I didn't know where I was going, I was just running. Everything was a blur. I didn't know where I was turning; I didn't look at street signs or count my steps or anything. I didn't even pay attention to traffic lights -- I just ran across the intersections without even looking. I don't know how long I ran, but all of a sudden I heard a car honking its horn at me. It kept honking, so finally I looked at it, and it was an old beat up gray Chevy, a Corsica, or one of those small cars from the 90s. It pulled over next to me, and I stopped and the driver reached over and lowered the window on the passenger side.

It was that guy I met at the funeral, Ryan Frazier. He looked worried.

"Are you all right?" he said. "You ran right through that

intersection and you almost got hit by a bus. I was on the cross street waiting for the light. I followed you, because you looked like you saw a ghost. Is something wrong?"

I leaned against a building, trying to catch my breath, and then I sat down on the sidewalk. I tried to talk, but all that came out were squeaky little chirps, and I couldn't make my voice work. Ryan got out of the car and came over and sat down next to me.

"What's wrong?" he said. "Are you all right? Can I do anything for you? Do you need help?"

I tried to answer all his questions, but still nothing came out except those noises.

Finally, he helped me to my feet and led me to his car. He put me in the passenger seat and then went around to the driver's side and started the car, and he drove to the parking lot of a Dunkin' Donuts and pulled in, and turned the motor off.

"Just breathe deeply," he said. "You'll be okay. Just calm down and tell me what happened."

It took me a long time, but finally I got my breath and I was able to speak. "My rabbit," I said. "Somebody killed it. Somebody killed my pet rabbit."

"Killed your rabbit?" he said. "What do you mean?"

"I have a pet rabbit. I keep him in my apartment. When I'm at work, he stays in his little house in the kitchen. I came home from work today, and he was. . . " I stopped. It was too hard to go on.

"He was what?" Ryan said.

"Killed," I said.

"How do you know someone killed him?"

"Because he had a butcher knife right through his chest," I shouted. "That's how I know."

"God, that's horrible," Ryan said. "Why would someone do that? Do you have any idea?"

"No."

"Do you have any enemies? Anyone who'd want to scare you?"

"I don't understand what you mean," I said. "Why would anyone want to scare me?"

"Maybe someone is angry at you."

"Why?" I said. "I haven't done anything to make someone angry at me."

"Well, I'm just trying to understand," Ryan said. "I mean, this just happened out of the blue? That's weird."

Then I remembered something. "I did have something strange happen this afternoon," I said. "I came back from the coffee shop after I left you, and there was a note taped to my computer. It said, 'YOU ARE EVIL AND YOU WILL BE PUNISHED,' in those stick-on letters you find at Staples.

Ryan whistled. "Wow, it sure seems like somebody is messing with your mind. You don't know who it could be?"

"No."

"Wait a minute," he said. "Didn't you tell me that guy who was your boyfriend, who killed the woman in the hotel, that he got away? They never caught him?"

"That's right," I said. "They never caught him."

"Do you think it's him?"

"Why would it be him?" I said. "I don't understand why he'd come back and kill my rabbit. What would that prove? It would be dangerous to come back when he's wanted for a crime. People would recognize him."

"I don't know," Ryan said. "It's hard to figure how somebody like that thinks. What was he like? What kind of a relationship did you have? Is there some unfinished business?"

"I don't know what you mean about unfinished business," I said.

"I mean was he mad at you for something, did he have a grudge?"

"Why would he be mad?" I said. "I did not do anything bad to him. Besides, it was a long time ago. I don't like thinking about it. I told you, things went bad for him. He wanted to impress people around here, but then his business went bad, and he started drinking, and he yelled a lot. He wanted me to have another lottery dream, but I couldn't do it. Maybe he was annoyed with me, I don't know."

"Annoyed enough to come back and hurt you?"

"How should I know?" I said. "I don't know about

something like that. I can't figure out why people are angry. It never makes sense to me."

"I think you shouldn't go back to your apartment," he said. "I think you should go to the police and report this, and then stay somewhere else."

"I'm not going to the police," I said. "I had enough of them when Perry got in trouble. They suspected that I was part of it for awhile. No, I'm not doing that. And I have to go back and get Charly and bury him somewhere. I can't just leave him there."

"Well, then I'm coming with you," he said. "I can't let you go back by yourself. Come on, I'll take you."

So Ryan drove me back and he helped me clean up the mess, and we buried Charly in the backyard of the apartment building.

After we buried Charly, Ryan came upstairs and I gave him some leftover pizza and I ate my sandwich. He kept asking me if I was scared, and I said no.

"If it's Perry, I am especially not scared," I said. "I was never scared of him. I think he is just mixed up. He had a hard life, and he gets angry about it and he shouts and sometimes throws things. He tries to fit in with people, but he's different, he never feels like he belongs. I am the same way about not belonging and I think he liked that about me, because it made us the same. I was different than other women."

"Why?" Ryan said. It seemed like he was trying to figure out a puzzle. "Why would you stay with somebody like that?"

"Because he understood me. And I understood him. He was

122

very simple: he just wanted people to say he was special. I knew that the first time I met him. He was like a bird with a damaged wing, and it flies around in circles. He was always flying around in circles, he couldn't leave his nest."

"But didn't you think he was dangerous? I mean, he killed someone."

"Yes, he was dangerous, but everybody is dangerous in some way. With him, it was just all out front. It was easier for me to read him than other people. I can't figure out most people, but I figured him out."

"Why do you think he would be stalking you?" Ryan said. He was really trying to figure this out, and I appreciated that he was so concerned.

"I don't know," I said. "Usually I can work him out, but not this time."

"But what if he hurts you?"

"I don't know if he will. But I will just have to see what happens."

Ryan wanted to stay the night but I wouldn't let him. I felt awkward about it, since I just met him. I shooed him off at 11:00 PM, and I told him not to worry about me.

"I will worry," he said. "And as a matter of fact, I'm going to sit in my car in the parking lot. I want you to call me on your cell phone if anything suspicious happens."

"You don't have to do that," I said.

"I want to do it," he said.

So, I let him do it. He wouldn't leave until he checked in every closet and under my bed and anywhere a stalker could hide. When he was satisfied, I said goodbye to him and then I locked up and got ready for bed.

It took me a long time to get to sleep, but finally I did and I had a strange dream.

I was in a place that was all white, and it was hard to hear. There was strange music playing, but it seemed to be close and far away at the same time. I couldn't tell where it was coming from. I felt like I was home, like something was familiar about it, but it was also a strange place, not like home at all. I didn't know what I was supposed to be doing there. Then my rabbit Charly came hopping by. I went over to pick him up and stroke his fur, but before I could get there, Perry appeared out of the whiteness. He was fatter now, with a blotchy red face and a beard and he had teeth missing. He had tattoos on him and he looked different. His hair was thinner, cut shorter. He looked at me and smiled, showing his missing teeth.

"I've been looking for you," he said.

And then I woke up. I was covered in sweat, and my heart was pounding, and it took me a while to calm down. I got up and went across to the window and looked out, and I could see Ryan's Chevy in the yellow cone of light from one of the lamps in my parking lot. It made me calmer to see him there, and I went back to bed.

In the morning I looked out again and the car was still there. I tapped on the window when I left for work, and Ryan opened the window and said, "Are you all right?"

"Yes," I said. "Thank you for staying all night, but you didn't have to do that."

"Yes I did," he said. "I was worried about you."

I thought about that when I walked down the street to my office. I didn't know if anyone really worried about me, so it was kind of nice. Perry never worried about me, I was sure of that. He was too wrapped up in his own world to think about anyone else very much. I decided Ryan was a good man.

I stopped and looked for my hawk before I went in the office, and he was in his tree, surveying his domain. He was the king of the area, and just seeing him there made it all right to go to work. Nothing bad could happen while he was there.

I unlocked the door and looked around my office, wondering if I'd find anything unusual. Nothing seemed different, so I sat down and started working on my computer.

CHAPTER EIGHTEEN

The day went by quickly, and before I knew it I heard a knock on my office door, and when I answered it I saw Ryan Frazier standing there, his big body taking up the whole doorway. "Are you ready to go to the silent movie theater?" he said.

"I'm sorry, I forgot," I said. "I don't want to go now. I have too much work to do."

"But I'd really be happy if you'd go with me," he said. His voice had a pleading tone, so I said, "Okay. Give me a minute, and I'll close up."

We drove along the river in his Chevy, and it was one of those days where you can't talk because it's so beautiful. The sky was a shade of blue like a jewel, and the light was everywhere, because it was winter and there were no leaves on the trees. It seemed like there was no shade anywhere, and I felt warm in the car even though it was bitter cold outside.

Greenton was a quaint little town on the upper Delaware, an hour's drive north of New Hope. It had jewel box houses and big Victorian mansions and quaint little bed and breakfast places, and the whole place reminded me of a community of doll houses. The main street had candy stores and a restored soda fountain and bicycle shops and little markets. We pulled up in front of a fancy old movie theater that looked like it had been built 100 years ago. It said, "The Grande Cinema" in big script letters out front, and there were old movie posters from the 1920s, advertising comedies and romances.

Inside, the theater was like something out of the early 1900s.

It had red velvet seats with brass trim, a big red curtain that stretched from floor to ceiling, carved oak panels on the walls and a mural on the ceiling with scenes from silent movies. It was like a church, or a cathedral, it seemed to me. A thirtyish man with his hair parted in the middle and a handlebar mustache, wearing a black vest and a string tie, came up the aisle to meet us.

"Hello, you must be the organist, Frazier, right?" he said, holding out his hand. "Glad to meet you. Name's Winston Bordeaux, at your service. I'm the manager, chairman of the board, chief cook and bottle washer in this emporium."

"Hello," Ryan said, shaking his hand. "This is my friend Rosalie Morley."

"Hello," I said. He held out his hand, but I never shake hands, so I just smiled. I noticed, though, that his fingers were long and graceful, like a piano player's.

"Well, let's get down to business," Mr. Bordeaux said. "Come on, let me show you the instrument."

He led the way down the aisle to an organ that was off to the side of the stage, and Ryan whistled when he saw it. It was all polished wood and brass and chrome, with pipes of various lengths sticking out from the top and back of it. It had three different keyboards, and lots of buttons with different labels on them. Ryan and Mr. Bordeaux chatted for awhile about the make and model of the organ, and Mr. Bordeaux told him how the non-profit foundation that ran the theater bought this old instrument from a theater in Canada that had closed ten years before, and they'd had to do thousands of dollars of restoration work on it.

Finally, Ryan said, "I'd really like to try it out, if you don't mind."

"By all means," Mr. Bordeaux said. "Help yourself. I'll step up to the projection room and start getting the film ready."

"It's 'Safety Last', with Harold Lloyd, right?" Ryan said.

"That's the one," Mr. Bordeaux said.

I sat down in the row of seats directly across from Ryan, and I watched as he tested the different sounds the organ could make. I don't normally look at people's faces, but I looked at him, and he had a big wide smile on his face. Sometimes he would close his eyes, or shake his head, and it seemed like he was in another world, so happy to be making sounds come out of that great instrument.

The organ definitely produced sounds that seemed to come from some special place. It could produce all sorts of sounds: heavenly chimes, brassy trumpets, breathy woodwinds, plucking strings, everything on the scale all the way down to a rumbling bass that I could feel in my bones. It wasn't just music, though -- the organ could make all sorts of other sounds, like hands clapping, glass breaking, honking horns, whistles, bird calls, a foghorn, a siren -- it seemed like it could make thousands of sounds.

After awhile Mr. Bordeaux came back and Ryan said the organ was working perfectly, and that he would like to get started. Mr. Bordeaux opened the curtain and there was a big movie screen behind it. Then he went back up the aisle to the projection room in the back of the theater, and he started the film.

"This is a comedy," Ryan said to me. "The star is a guy named Harold Lloyd." The movie came on, and Ryan talked to me while it played. "That's Harold Lloyd," he said. "The guy in the glasses. He gets into a lot of pickles. Just watch what happens."

This tall skinny man with glasses named Harold Lloyd certainly did get into a lot of crazy situations. Ryan played along, making the organ almost talk or sing if the moment called for it, and what he did on the organ made it easier for me to figure out what was going on in the movie. I didn't see the humor in it, because this Harold Lloyd fellow kept getting into dangerous situations, like the one where he was hanging high above a city street holding on to the hands of a large clock, and I kept waiting for him to fall down and get run over by a car or a bus. Ryan was making funny noises on the organ, and I could tell I was supposed to laugh at this point, but all I could think was how many feet Harold Lloyd would fall if he let go of those clock hands.

When the comedy short was finished Ryan played some tunes on the organ while Mr. Bordeaux loaded the projector with the next film. Ryan explained that this was standard in silent movies theaters in the old days. People went to see several movies, hear an organ concert, and maybe watch a few live acts, he said. "It was a whole evening of entertainment," he said.

After the comedy short, Mr. Bordeaux played the full length movie. This was a drama called "The Passion Of Joan Of Arc", starring someone named Renee Falconetti. Ryan got to play different kinds of music for this movie. It was a drama about Joan of Arc, and it was fascinating, mostly because Ryan's organ playing was so wrapped up with the facial expressions of the actors. It was amazing to me -- I felt like I could understand what they were thinking. There were many close-ups of Renee Falconetti, and her face showed so many emotions that I was hypnotized by it. I got so caught up in it that by the end, when Joan was burned at the stake, I actually cried for the first time in years. I was shocked by my reaction to the movie.

Afterward, Mr. Bordeaux walked down the aisle and told Ryan he'd done an excellent job, and he was hired to play at the upcoming film festival. Ryan seemed pleased at this, and when we went outside he wanted to take me for a coffee. The sun had set, but the sky still had some light in it, and you could see the stars just starting to come out in the Western corner of the sky.

We found a coffee shop and got some hot coffee. We took our coffees and walked along the main street for awhile.

"Did you enjoy the movies?" Ryan said.

"I liked your playing," I said. "And yes, the movies were good. I don't usually go to the movies or watch TV, because I have a hard time understanding what's going on. It was easier with the silent movies, though. I could follow it better. I think it was your playing that helped. And the people's faces were easier to make sense of."

"Good," he said. "I'm glad."

When we finished our coffees we got back in Ryan's car and drove home. Ryan was quiet for awhile, but then he started talking. "I'm glad I moved here," he said. "I already like this place. I like my teaching job, I like where I'm living, and I like that I'm going to get a chance to be involved with that theater. And I like that I met you."

"That's nice," I said.

He laughed. "Don't feel any obligation to say anything nice to me, just because I said I like that I met you."

"No," I said. "I won't. But I will say it if you want me to."

"No, no," he said, laughing again. "I don't want to force you."

"This has been a nice afternoon," I said. "Is that what you want me to say? It's not untrue for me to say that."

"Good," he said. "I don't want you to say anything untrue."

Just then my phone rang, and I answered it. I didn't usually get calls this time of night, and I didn't recognize the number on the screen, but I answered anyway.

There was a silence, then, "Where are you?"

"Who is this?" I said.

"You will find out," it said. Then the person hung up.

CHAPTER NINETEEN

I put the phone down and looked out the window.

"What's wrong?" Ryan said.

"Nothing," I said. "I don't want to talk about it." It was night now, and I looked out the window at the lights of the towns we passed on our way home. Here and there I saw people talking in the halo from a street lamp, or the glow from a store window. It was like scenes strung together in a long chain, moments frozen in time.

"Did you like the movie?" Ryan said, finally.

"Yes," I said. "It was interesting. I enjoyed it very much. I could understand what the actors were thinking, just by looking at them."

"I'm glad," Ryan said. "It's considered a classic film. I like the way silent movies convey so much emotion by the way they use light and shadow. Do you know, I read that F.W. Murnau, a famous silent film director, said that it was a shame talking pictures were invented when they were. He said, "We were just learning how to make movies. When sound movies were developed, all of a sudden the films became like theater, with so much talking." It's interesting to think that movies could have developed differently if sound hadn't been added for another twenty years."

"What's the use of thinking that?" I said. "They invented the technology to add sound to films, and that's that. It's just fantasizing, what you're doing."

"I guess I like to ask 'What if' questions sometimes," Ryan

said.

"Not me," I said. "I'm only interested in what's happening now, not what could have been."

He laughed. "I can see that." Then he turned to me and lowered his voice. "You seem troubled, though. Is anything wrong?"

"I don't know how you would come up with an idea like that," I said. "How would you know if I am troubled? You can't read my mind."

"Well, that phone call seemed to make you very quiet all of a sudden. To me, that means something about the phone call troubled you."

"You're guessing a lot about me," I said. "You shouldn't make guesses like that. It's not logical. You're just associating my behavior with something that happened about the same time, the phone call. It's not a logical connection."

"There are different kinds of logic," he said. "There's a logic of emotions."

"Oh, please," I said. "That doesn't make sense at all. You are just babbling on now, Ryan. Please leave me alone; I don't want to talk anymore."

"As you wish," he said.

We drove in silence the rest of the way home. When we pulled into the parking lot of my building, I thanked Ryan and started to get out.

"But wait," he said. "Can I come in?"

"Why?" I said.

"Maybe someone is in there. Don't you want me to come inside with you to check things out?"

"No," I said. "I will be fine. Thank you for a pleasant evening. I want to go inside now."

Being around people tires me out, and all I wanted to do was go inside and relax with my bird books. Ryan was acting strange, because he walked me to my door and kept saying, "Are you sure? Shouldn't I come in?"

"I am sure," I said. "I don't need you to come in. I just want to go upstairs and relax."

"But what about your rabbit?" he said. "Aren't you worried that whoever killed your rabbit will come back?"

"I am not worried," I said. "If it is Perry, I can handle him. I am not afraid of him."

"Okay," he said, exhaling as if he had been holding his breath forever. He put his hand on my shoulder, and I drew back, because I don't really like people touching me. "I just want you to be okay," he said. "I don't want anything to happen to you."

"Nothing will happen to me," I said, and I stepped across the threshold and closed the door behind me.

I went upstairs and down the hall to my apartment, and I let myself in. Everything seemed normal when I got inside. All I wanted to do was take a shower and relax with my bird books. I went into the bedroom and took off my pants, my shirt and shoes and everything else, and I ran a hot shower. I stayed in there a long time and let the hot water run across my body. I like hot showers, because they make me feel clean and refreshed. I like the patterns of the water on the shower door, and sometimes I just stand there and watch that. The water beads are like little jewels in the light, and I like to imagine they're little diamonds, thousands of little diamonds.

When I got out I dried myself with a fluffy white towel and then I put my white terrycloth bathrobe on and brushed my hair and came out of the bathroom. I was going to get myself a glass of orange juice, and I went over to the refrigerator, and that's when I saw the note on my refrigerator door. It was on the same kind of yellow legal paper as the note on my computer the other day, only this time it was written in block letters, the way a child would do. It was stuck to the door with Scotch tape, and when I pulled it off the top of the paper ripped. I had to put it back together carefully to read it.

"You have an appointment with me," it said.

I was sure that note wasn't there when I came in. Someone must have put it there when I was taking a shower. I went around the apartment and checked everywhere, even in the smallest spaces, in all the closets and under the bed and everywhere, and I checked the door and the windows. There was a window in the living room that was open a crack, and I figured that's how the person got in. They climbed in the window and then climbed back out again and closed the window. I looked out and although the window was on the second floor, I didn't see a ladder anywhere. The person somehow got up to the second floor and through the window, but they'd gotten away and taken their ladder with them.

I sat down on the couch and thought about this. Someone

was obviously stalking me, and leaving these puzzling notes. Could it be Perry? I wondered why he would do something like that. We had our problems, but I thought he understood me and I understood him. Maybe I was wrong. It wouldn't be the first time I was wrong about someone. People were hard to figure out. People were definitely very complicated beings. I don't think birds stalk each other. It's not like they're always peaceful, though. I know that. I am sure my hawk has eaten other, smaller birds as well as mice and other small animals. That's what hawks do. They are predators. They have to eat to survive, and they eat other birds sometimes. That's just life.

I picked up one of my bird books from the bookcase and I started paging through it. It always calms me to read about birds. I love reading facts about them, like how many sounds a bird can make. Birds have an organ called a syrinx, which helps them make a wider variety of sounds than humans can make. The Australian lyrebird can make thousands of sounds, including the sound of a digital camera and a chainsaw. I think it would be great to make that many sounds.

So I lost myself in the book for awhile, just paging through it and looking at the birds. I just love thinking about what it would be like to fly above the treetops, to get a view of the world from that perspective. I love that birds have better vision, smell and hearing than us. Like, how a hawk can be hundreds of feet in the air and see a tiny field mouse poking around in the grass somewhere. It's really amazing, and I wish I could see like that. I also wish I could just fly from place to place whenever I wanted to. I love reading about sea birds that fly for days at a time when they're migrating, or the way birds can get trapped in hurricanes and be blown hundreds of miles off course. Bird watchers will head to the coast whenever a hurricane passes by, because they sometimes will see birds that are native to France or England pecking about in the dunes at the Jersey Shore.

I couldn't get lost in the pictures tonight, though. Somehow I couldn't shake the feeling that something wasn't right. I was restless, distracted. That's when the phone rang and I saw that strange phone number again.

"Who is it?" I said.

There was silence.

"Is this Perry?" I said. "Why are you bothering me? Why did you come back?"

"I have your hawk," the voice said.

CHAPTER TWENTY

It was Perry, I was sure of that now.

"What do you mean, Perry?" I said. "What are you talking about?"

"I know you like to watch the hawk down by the river. I know which one it is. I caught him."

"That's impossible," I said. "He flies too high."

"I caught him," the voice said. "I'm good at catching animals. I had to learn that after I left."

"Perry, stop holding your hand over the phone," I said. "I know it's you. You have to stop this. You are wanted for murder, and the police are looking for you. You should not be bothering me."

"If you want to see your hawk, come to the top of the Holicong Mountain, by the old church."

"What are you talking about?"

"Come to the mountain. Now."

Then the phone went dead.

Now I knew for sure it was Perry. He and I used to go to the top of Holicong Mountain, which wasn't really a mountain but a sort of steep hill that was like a forested bump on the countryside, and we'd walk among this old graveyard where there were African Americans buried whose ancestors came up from the South during slave times. This place was a stop on the Underground Railroad, and it had a lot of history to it. The mountain was mostly deserted now; there were only a few houses back in the woods with people in them, so we always felt we had it to ourselves. There was a little Baptist church there and it only opened once a year, on Christmas Eve, for a service.

I didn't think anybody else knew or cared much about that place, because we never saw anyone there. That's why it had to be Perry on the phone, because he was the only person who knew about the place. I couldn't believe that he had my hawk, but I had to find out what was going on, so I decided to go. I put on some jeans and a sweater, and slipped on some sandals and got my car keys and went out. It was almost dusk outside; the sun was almost down and there was a fading orange light in the sky. I got in the car and drove the way I knew to the Holicong Mountain, through Lahaska on Route 263 and then turning left onto Holicong road.

The road up the mountain was a winding one, and as usual there was nobody on it. The sun shone through the trees, making a latticework effect, with fiery gold and orange light in patterns on the landscape. I got to the top of the mountain where the little wooden church was, and I saw that the red wooden door was halfway open. I parked my car next to the church and got out. I didn't see a car anywhere, but there was definitely somebody inside the church. There was a light on inside.

I walked up the three steps to the church, and I pushed the door wide. Inside, there were only about a dozen wooden pews, and I saw someone sitting in the first pew, with his back to me. As I came in the door he turned and I saw enough of his face to know that it was Perry, although he had changed. I didn't look too closely but I could tell his face was puffier, red and blotchy, and his hair

139

was thin on top. He looked like he'd gained about 25 pounds. He was wearing an Amy fatigue jacket and pants, and he had a thick brown mustache now.

"Hello Rosalie," he said, turning all the way around. He grinned and I could see he had some teeth missing. There was a scar running along his cheek too. That had never been there before. I didn't want to keep looking at his face, but I was so surprised at all the changes in him that I couldn't take my eyes away.

"Perry, what are you doing here?" I said. "And why are you stalking me?"

He smiled again. "I wanted to see you, Rosalie. Is there something wrong with that?"

"You're wanted by the police," I said. "You ran away. If you're here, you should go turn yourself in to them. That's the right thing to do."

He laughed, but it didn't sound much like laughter. Not the kind of laughter that means you're happy, anyway. This was like dragging a piece of chalk over a blackboard.

"I bet you'd like that, wouldn't you?" he said. "Turn myself in -- that would suit you, wouldn't it? Then they'd fry me, or just put me away for life, which is the same thing. Can't you just see the headlines? 'Perry Lukens, who was once an up and comer, a man who was going places, is on trial for the murder of a local woman.' I'd have to go through all that shame and humiliation, in front of all the people who used to think I was somebody special. Oh, that would be sweet, wouldn't it?'

"No it would not be sweet," I said. "It would be sad, but it's the right thing to do."

"Sad?" he yelled, and his voice echoed in the small church. "What do you know about sad? You don't know anything about that, Rosalie. You don't feel anything, do you? You're like a stone, or maybe a robot. You're all about numbers, patterns, collecting and sorting. You never cared about me. I bet you haven't lost any sleep since what happened to me, have you? You love your damn animals more than you ever loved me!"

"That's not true," I said. "I cared for you, Perry. I thought we had something special. I thought you understood me, and I understood you. I still care for you. I don't just stop loving people when they do something wrong. But when you do something wrong, you have to pay for it. That's just the rules. You did something wrong -- you killed that woman. You have to pay -- it's all about justice."

"Justice?" he said, and his face twisted into a smile again. "That's a laugh. There ain't no justice, Rosalie. If there were justice, I wouldn't have been raised up the way I was. I wouldn't have had that bitch for a mother. If there were justice, she would have paid for what happened to me. I started out this life with two strikes against me, and that ain't fair."

"I'm sorry for what happened to you," I said. "But it doesn't change the fact that you killed somebody. That's not right, Perry."

"That Margo woman was like an animal, coming on to me, stalking me," he said, his voice echoing in the church. "I didn't have a chance." He laughed, and it sounded like a machine gun firing. I never heard him laugh like that, and it suddenly dawned on me that he must be high or drunk. He was jumpy, shifting his weight from one foot to the other, and his eyes were glittery and big. "I'm just a simple country boy, Rosalie," he said, laughing again. "I don't understand these big city women."

"Is that supposed to be a joke?" I said. "Because I don't understand it."

"No joke," he said, walking down the aisle. "I know you never understood jokes, Rosalie, so I wouldn't even try to joke with you."

The floorboards creaked with every step he took. I looked down and saw that he had black motorcycle boots on. He must have ridden a motorcycle up the mountain and hid it in the bushes. I noticed drops of blood on the boots, and then I looked closer and saw that he had one hand behind his back.

"Perry," I said. "Why do you have one hand behind your back?"

He walked right up to me, so close I could smell his rotten breath, and he said, "Because I wanted to show you something."

And then he grabbed me by the shoulder with one hand, and with the other hand he held something up to my face.

All I saw at first was a mass of feathers, but then I saw the dead eyes and the head twisted at a crazy angle.

It was my hawk.

"Perry, why did you--"

In a flash, Perry dropped the hawk and pulled out a knife, then held it to my throat. I felt the point of the knife prick the skin right under my jawline, and I froze.

"You want to know why I killed your precious hawk, don't you?" he shouted. "Because I want to hurt you, that's why. See, I decided that you're evil, Rosalie. Oh, yeah, I figured it all out. I had a lot of time for thinking, these last five years. It ain't easy for somebody like me to find work, not when I have so much to hide. I've had to move around a lot, just to keep folks from getting suspicious. I don't live in a big fancy house or go out to dinner in nice restaurants now. No, I do odd jobs for people just to make a few dollars, and I live in cheap motels. So, I spend a lot of time drinking and thinking, just drinking and thinking. And I figured out that you're a witch, Rosalie. A damn witch, you and your lottery dreams."

"Perry, you don't mean that," I said. "You can't."

"Oh yes I can," he said. His breath stank of cheap wine, a sweet, rotten smell.

"I'm not a witch," I said. "I don't know why you would say that."

"I say it because it's true!" he shouted in my face. "You know, when I figure it all out, I realize that my life went downhill as soon as I met you. Oh, things seemed good for awhile. I was making money, moving ahead, strutting around like a big man. But those dreams you had, Rosalie, they were weird. I mean, who dreams the winning numbers in the lottery? Huh? That just doesn't happen. You won me all that money, and I thought I was finally gonna make it, finally show my bitch mother that I could be somebody, but then it got snatched all away. Remember? Everything just disappeared!"

He swayed a bit, but then he pressed the blade in harder.

"Perry, you're hurting me," I said.

"Ha! See how it feels," he said. "That's the way I felt for two years, when my life started to fall apart. Just like I had a knife sticking in my neck and I couldn't move any which way without getting cut. There was no way out, and I felt trapped. But then I thought: why, of course there's a way out. I'll just ask Rosalie to dream me one of them dreams again. Just dream another winning lottery number, and then I'll get out of this mess. But you wouldn't do that, would you?"

"I couldn't," I said. "I told you, I didn't have any control over those dreams. They just happened."

"Sure, sure," he said. "That's what you told me. It was out of your control. But I think you were playing with me, babe. See, it seems to me that you did have control, because you dreamed those dreams in the first place. You just wanted to have some fun with Perry, toy with him a bit, see him squirm. Because when I needed you the most, you didn't come through. I needed that money bad, Rosalie, and you didn't come through. You left me hanging."

"I didn't do it on purpose," I said. "I couldn't make those dreams happen again. I told you, I don't have control of them."

"Wrong answer!" he said, pushing the point of the knife just a bit harder. "No, I think it's because you're evil," he said. "You're a witch, Rosalie, that's what it is. I figured it out!"

"Do you hear yourself, Perry?" I said. "You're not talking any sense. Why don't you put the knife down and we can talk about this?"

"What's there to talk about?" he said. "There's no discussion. You're a witch, and that's all there is to it. You deserve to die, like all witches. When I kill you I'll release the curse you've put on me, and my life will get better."

"I did not put any curse on you," I said. "Put the knife down and we can talk."

"No," he said. "I have a better idea. I'm going to do what they do to all witches. I'm going to burn you at the stake."

At first I did not think I heard him correctly. I could not imagine Perry doing something like that, burning me at the stake. It did not seem like the Perry I knew.

But he was different than the Perry I remembered. He seemed to want to make me uncomfortable, standing only inches from my face and grinning, breathing on me with his smelly breath. I kept my eyes down, looking down at the rough skin on his fingers, his dirty fingernails, and the frayed cuffs of his flannel shirt. He brought his free hand up and grabbed my hair, and slowly pulled my head back so that I was forced to look at him.

"You don't like looking at me, do you?" he said. His breath really stank, and his teeth were brown and stained, with a couple of them missing. His eyes were bloodshot, and his hair looked like he hadn't washed it in weeks. I tried to look away, but he kept pulling my head back so that I had to look at him.

"Look at my face!" he said. "You are the worst thing that ever happened to me, worse than even that goddamned mother of mine. Everything would have been okay if I hadn't ever met you. You were sent by the Devil to torment me, to ruin my life, and you did."

I couldn't help but look at him, and it was like I was seeing him for the first time. Who was this person standing in front of me?

I didn't recognize him at all. I hadn't looked into his eyes in a long time, maybe never, but now I did.

I did not like what I saw. There was hurt in them, and anger. A deeper anger than I had ever experienced, and it made me shiver.

"You don't like what you see, do you?" he said, cackling. "It's the look of justice, Rosalie. Justice for you, for your evil ways. You're going to pay now for what you did to me. You're goddam going to pay."

He yanked on my head and prodded me with the knife. "Come on, we're going outside. Move!"

I did not have a choice now. He pulled and prodded me toward the back door, and we went out the door and down the steps. Then he yanked me along to a place in the middle of the graveyard, where there was a big old tree right in the middle of the gravestones. Even though it was completely dark now, there was a full moon shining through the trees, and it lit up the graveyard enough that I could see pretty well.

Perry was pushing me along so fast that I stumbled across the uneven ground.

As we got closer I could see that the tree had a pile of trash and leaves at its base, and then I smelled something: gasoline.

"What is this?" I said. "What are you doing?"

"Just what I told you," he said. "I got things set up all nice here, everything just right to burn you to a crisp, Rosalie."

He pulled me over and made me stand by the tree, and then

146

pushed me up against it and said, "Put your hands around the back of this tree trunk."

"Think about what you're doing, Perry," I said. "You do not really want to do this, do you?"

He laughed, and it was an ugly sound. "I want to do it more than anything I've done. I'm going to get rid of the curse you put on me, babe. Get rid of it for good. And everything will be better once you're gone."

He put the knife between his teeth and used both hands to pull my hands around the back of the tree, and then he reached in the pocket of his Army jacket and pulled out some rope. He worked fast, and in no time he had my hands tied so tight that my wrists hurt. He bound them to the tree trunk, and there was no way I could move. Then he bent down and tied my ankles just as tightly.

When he was finished he stood up and admired his work. "Not bad, huh?" he said. "I've had to live outside a lot these past years, and I've learned how to do a good job of tying things. I'm a regular mountain man!" he cackled.

The stink of gasoline was overpowering, and since my feet were in the pile of trash, they were in the middle of it. The gas was seeping into my shoes now.

"Are you scared, witch?" Perry said.

"You should stop calling me a witch," I said. "I am not a witch. I told you that."

"You're a damn witch!" he said, and he cackled again. "Are you scared?" he repeated.

"No," I said.

"I should have figured that," he said. "You don't have any feelings, do you? You're not a person, you're a copy of a person. You're a robot or something. Well, let's see how well you burn."

There was a big stick about twice the size of a baseball bat lying in the trash at my feet, and Perry picked it up. I could see that it had a lump of cloth twisted around one end, and I could smell gasoline on it. He took a lighter out of his pocket and lit the end of the stick.

"What do you think?" he said, holding the torch up beneath his face, so it gave him a ghoulish look. "Do I look scary? Well, I'd be scared if I was you, Rosalie."

I don't react like most people to situations like this. Maybe I don't feel the way other people do, but my body reacts in its own way. My legs got weak, and I started shivering all over. I was shaking like I was standing outside naked in zero degree weather. I couldn't control the shivering, and then my teeth started chattering. Perry was jumping around, doing some weird dance and cackling like a madman. The thought occurred to me that I would not see my family anymore, and it seemed strange, like if the sun came up in the middle of the night.

And then something weird happened. I heard a noise, and there was a white light, and all of a sudden I was surrounded by lots of people. I saw them walking around me in the woods, and I thought at first they were the spirits of the dead African Americans in the graveyard. Then I saw some familiar faces, like my grandmother Rosie and Jack Caldwell, and I realized these were my dead family. I saw people with Irish faces, some of them dressed in old-fashioned clothing, the women in long black dresses and shawls and the men with floppy hats, some of them smoking pipes. They were walking around me, wandering all around, and they would walk right past Perry with his torch and not even look at him.

They were coming to me.

CHAPTER TWENTY ONE

I saw them walk right up to me and smile, and the look on their faces gave me a shock.

It's because I could understand exactly what they were feeling, and it was the first time I had ever known something like that just from looking at someone's face.

Their faces were filled with what I suddenly understood was kindness and love, and one of them, an old woman with a shock of white hair and warm dark eyes, walked up to me and she touched me on the shoulder with her hand. Right then the shaking in my body stopped, and I was calm, so calm. She smiled at me and then kept walking in circles like the rest of them.

It was like one of my strange dreams, only I was wide awake. It was strange and dreamlike, but somehow I felt all those people were looking out for me, and I felt a connection with them. They were family.

Perry was still dancing around, but he was weaving closer to me, and I knew he was getting ready to put the torch down and light the pile of trash at my feet. My shaking had stopped, though, and I just watched him calmly.

All of a sudden, I saw something big and heavy come out of the dark and plow into Perry, and he went tumbling down, and the torch ended up yards away in a pile of wet leaves.

It was hard to see what was going on, because Perry was almost out of my field of vision. For a moment I thought it was one of the people in my waking dream who'd knocked him down. Then I heard a familiar voice.

"Rosalie, are you all right?"

It was Ryan Frazier. He was on the ground near where he'd knocked Perry down. I couldn't see him very well, but I heard him.

"I'm fine," I said. "What are you doing here?"

"It's a long story," he said, suddenly appearing in front of me, panting for breath. "I put a tracking device on your car. I'm sorry to do that, but I was worried for your safety. When you went out tonight, the beacon went off on my phone, and I tracked you here."

"I am glad you did," I said.

He came closer. "Let's get you untied and get out of here," he said. He started to go around behind me, but the next thing I knew there was a wild scream and a thudding sound and Ryan went tumbling down himself. I saw Perry then, holding a heavy stick, and it was obvious that is what he used to knock Ryan down.

"So, your boyfriend came to save you," he said, grinning. "I knew about him -- I followed you to that movie theater, and I even snuck in and watched that stupid old movie, from a row in the back. I could have killed you both then, but I waited. Now, he'll just have to die with you."

He pulled a big knife out of his pocket, and ran his finger along the edge. "Good thing I sharpened it this morning," he said.

Ryan was moaning on the ground, groggy from being hit in the head, and I knew I had to wake him up.

151

"Ryan," I screamed. "Get up! He's got a knife."

It was too late, Perry pounced on him, and they started rolling around on the ground. I saw Perry raise his arm, the knife blade gleamed in the moonlight, and I thought it was over.

Ryan had more strength than I thought, though, and they rolled around punching and grappling with each other. They rolled out of the light and I could only see two black shapes at this point. Then they rolled back, and I saw that Perry was on top of Ryan, and I saw him raise the knife. Somehow Ryan's hand got free and he grabbed Perry's knife hand and held it fast. Then Ryan reached up with his other hand and grabbed Perry's ear and twisted it till I saw blood coming down from his fingers. Perry screamed and while he was distracted with pain Ryan shifted his weight under him and toppled him over. Now he was on top of Perry.

Ryan was a big man, and he had Perry pinned under him easily. He wrenched the knife from Perry's hand and threw it into the darkness. Perry screamed in rage, and he struggled hard to get free, flailing his fists at Ryan's face. He connected with one punch, which snapped Ryan's head back, but that didn't move his body. Ryan proceeded to pound Perry's face with one punch after another. He kept hitting and hitting, and I thought he'd kill Perry.

"Stop!" I screamed. "Ryan, stop it, you're going to kill him!"

Finally, Ryan stopped. He was breathing heavily, and his face was slick with sweat. Perry was motionless on the ground, his eyes half closed, his face covered in blood. He was moaning softly.

Ryan seemed to struggle to get control of himself, but finally he got off Perry, stood up and came over to me.

152

"Let's go home," he said, still panting, and he started to untie me.

When he got me free, I put my arms around him. It was something I'd never done with anyone before, spontaneously hugged them, and I certainly didn't plan it -- it just happened. Ryan hugged me back, and I felt his racing heart against my chest. He was trembling, too.

"I was so afraid you'd be hurt," he said.

"I am okay," I said. "He killed my hawk."

"He's dangerous," Ryan said. "We need to call the police on him. I left my phone in the car. Do you have your phone on you?"

"No," I said. "It's in my car."

"Okay, here's what we need to do," Ryan said. "I want you to go get your phone and call 911. Tell them to send the police here right away, because this guy tried to murder you. I'll wait here and make sure he doesn't go anywhere."

But it was already too late. There was a rustling noise, and when I turned to look, Perry had scrambled to his feet and was running off in the darkness. In a moment I saw a shadowy figure pick up the burning torch that was still lying 20 yards away where it landed after Ryan knocked it out of Perry's hand.

Perry had the torch. He stood there and held it in front of him, and it lit up his face like he was in some old-fashioned horror movie.

He looked terrible. Ryan had bloodied his face and knocked

out another tooth, and his lips were swollen. He was covered in dirt and blood, and his hair was wild. He was panting heavily, like he'd just run a marathon, and he was unsteady on his feet.

"Looks like you got rescued, Rosalie," he said. "I guess all good witches like you have a helper somewhere, right?"

"Perry, give it up," Ryan said. "You need to stop with this fantasy, and listen to reason."

"Reason?" Perry said, laughing. "That's funny. There ain't no reason in this at all. She's a witch, plain and simple, and she put a curse on me."

"Perry, I told you before, I am not a witch," I said. "I don't know why you keep saying that."

Perry moved closer. In the light from the torch he looked like some unearthly creature, some ghoul that belonged in the graveyard.

"You ruined my life," he said. "I just wanted to pay you back for that."

"I didn't do anything to your life," I said. "Whatever happened, you did it."

"Rosalie, stop," Ryan whispered. "Don't get him angrier."

"What's that?" Perry said, taking another step closer. "What's your fat boyfriend saying, babe? Don't want to get me angry? Is that it? Well, that's okay, you don't have to worry about anything. You won't get me angry. No, you don't have to worry about anything anymore. I won't hurt you, babe, or your stupid fat boyfriend. I'm done with all that."

"Perry, just calm down," Ryan said. "Everything is going to be okay. You're hurt. Let us get some help for you."

"Help?" Perry said, chuckling. "Oh, I bet you'd love to get some help for me. Yeah, I sure bet you would. You could get the cops to come and help me real good, right? Then they'd put me in jail and throw away the key. Oh, I bet you'd like that."

"We just want to help you," Ryan said.

"Well, I don't need your help," Perry said. "I don't need anybody's help anymore. I just had some bad luck, meeting up with this witch here, and now I got to just suck it up and do what's necessary."

"What do you mean?" I said.

"Oh, you'll see," he said. He was still weaving about, woozy, and with a strange grin on his face. "I'm so clumsy," he said, looking down at his clothes. "I spilled gasoline all over myself when I was getting things ready tonight. Such a stupid thing to do, isn't it?"

"Perry, what are you doing?" I said.

I saw the old, white-haired woman of my vision walk up behind him and put her hand on his shoulder.

I screamed.

He grinned, took the torch and touched it to the cuff of his pants.

"No!" Ryan shouted.

The flames leaped up like some living thing, and in an instant his clothes were on fire. He screamed, twisted and turned as the flames touched his skin, but he didn't roll on the ground to put them out. He seemed determined to stay upright.

For a moment I was frozen in place, watching this horrible scene, but then Ryan yelled, "No!" and leaped into action. He took off his coat and ran to Perry and I could see he wanted to wrap the coat around him, but the flames were getting higher every second, and Perry put out his hand and waved him off.

Ryan tried to get closer, but some of the flames leaped onto his coat, and he had to fall on the ground and start rolling around to put them out.

When he got the flames out he yelled, "Roll on the ground, Perry! Roll on the ground!"

But Perry didn't do it. He stumbled around the graveyard, holding his hands to his face as the flames leaped up, but he seemed determined not to fall down. We watched in horror as he lurched around, like some zombie creature from a horror movie, writhing spastically in pain but not making a sound. Finally, he fell, tripping on an exposed tree root and tumbling down a small hill, where he lay still as the flames consumed him. The smell of burning flesh was sickening, and I sank to my knees and vomited. Ryan did too, and when we recovered, the flames were tapering off. We sat there for a long time in shocked silence, watching the flames die down.

Then the darkness returned and we could see nothing, although the stench was even worse now.

* * *

It's been a year since Perry died in the flames.

For a long time I couldn't get that image out of my mind of him burning up. I kept waking up in the middle of the night and seeing it, and sometimes I even thought I was back there in the woods, and I smelled that horrible smell of burning flesh.

I did not actually see his body after he burned himself. Ryan went over to him and looked at him for a moment, and then he turned away. He came back holding his nose and said, "Let's go. He's dead. There's nothing we can do for him."

We went back to our cars and Ryan called the police, and we waited till they came up the mountain. Three patrol cars drove up and parked, and the flashing red lights lit up the graveyard and the little church, throwing eerie shapes and shadows all over it. The officers went over to look at the body, then came back with handkerchiefs over their faces and one of them threw up in the bushes behind the church.

They asked us a lot of questions, and when I told them the body was Perry Lukens, at first they didn't recognize the name. They were all young guys in their mid-20s and they weren't even on the force when Perry killed Margo. I had to explain the whole thing to them, and it wasn't till another cop showed up, an older man of about 40, that anybody knew what I was talking about.

"Sure, I remember that," the policeman said. "That was pretty gruesome. He got away, right? They never caught him."

"Yes," I said. "He got away. But then he came back."

"Why did he come back?" the policeman said.

"He wanted to kill me," I said.

I started to explain the story, that Perry seemed to think I was a witch, and he blamed me for all the troubles in his life, but they were looking at me funny, as if I was making everything up. Ryan broke in and said, "Listen, she's had a rough night. Can I take her home now? I'm sure she can come and answer any questions in the morning."

The policemen walked off a few paces and had a little meeting standing next to the wall of the church, and then the older one came back and said it was okay for us to leave, but I'd have to come in for questioning tomorrow morning.

Ryan followed me home in his car. When we got to my apartment I was about to go in, but then I thought I should invite Ryan in because he saved my life. He came upstairs and we made mugs of tea and sat on my couch and all of a sudden I started shaking again, till my whole body was shaking and I couldn't make it stop. Ryan put his arms around me and held me tight, and for once I didn't push him away. I felt strangely warm and calm in his arms, and I just sat there letting him rock me back and forth. We did not say anything for a long time. After a while I fell asleep, and somehow Ryan must have carried me into my bed, because I woke up the next morning in bed, and he was gone.

Ryan found a lawyer for me and we went in and answered all the questions the next day, and I made my statement, and the police were satisfied. The story was all over the news for a few days, but Ryan and the lawyer kept the reporters away, and I did not have to answer any of their questions.

After a few days I went back to work, and although people around town gave me some strange looks, nobody asked about Perry

158

or what happened. Ryan came to my office every day for lunch, and most of the time he came back at the end of the day and we took a drive to some little town on the Delaware and went out to dinner. Nobody recognized me when we went to these little New Jersey and Pennsylvania towns, so I got no funny looks or questions.

So, it faded away in time. Perry was gone, and I started to get on with my life. Ryan became a part of my routine, and whenever he was playing the organ at the silent movie theater, I went along to watch the movie and listen to him play. I got to where I really liked the silent movies, and I felt like just watching them helped me to figure out what people were doing when they made a facial expression. I studied the faces of the great comedians like Charlie Chaplin, and in time I could understand faces better. I was able to look at people's faces and I had a better idea of what they were really saying when they talked to me.

And Ryan showed me how the music was such an important part of the movie. I watched and listened, and I heard how he underlined and emphasized what was happening up on the screen, how the sounds from the organ were connected to the expressions on the actors' faces, what they said and did. I'd sit with him sometimes and he'd teach me how to play the organ, what all the pedals and buttons meant. Once he even let me play for a movie, and he told me afterward that I did a great job.

I spent a lot of time with Ryan, and I still do. I feel that we have a special feeling for each other. It's like the way I felt about Perry at one time, although now I know I never really knew Perry, and he didn't know me. Now that I have Ryan, I know what real togetherness is.

Oh, there's one more thing. In time the pictures of Perry,

those horrible pictures in my head, faded away. I didn't think much about that night anymore. It was like there was a blank spot in my head. Then one day, though, I was visiting my parents' house with Ryan, and my mother got out an old photo album. She was doing the family history, and when she finished with her side, she had started on my father's side. Anyway, she had found some pictures among Rosie's things that they cleaned out of her apartment years before when she died, and now she'd put them into an album. I was paging through it, when all of a sudden I stopped. There was a picture from a photographer's studio that my mom said was more than 100 years old, from before 1900, and it was of a woman in a long black dress and a bonnet with three little boys. Two of them were standing by her side, but the youngest, hardly more than a baby, was on her lap.

"That's your great great grandmother Rose Sullivan Morley," my mom said. "Those are her sons. The one on the right is your great grandfather Paul, who was your grandmother Rosie's father."

"I know her," I said, suddenly.

"Well, you're related to her," my mother said, "so you know she's part of your family tree."

"No, I know her," I said. "I saw her."

My mother looked at me with her eyes narrowed. "What do you mean? When did you see her?"

"That night," I said. "When Perry tried to kill me. I was tied to a tree in the church cemetery, and all of a sudden there were people walking all around me. I saw Rosie and Jack Caldwell, but most of the people I didn't know. Some of them were wearing old-fashioned clothes. I was sure they were related to me, though. I was

160

sure they were my family. And that woman," I pointed to the picture. "She was there. She smiled at me, and I knew everything was going to be all right."

After that I wanted to find out more about my family history, and my mother told me where my great grandmother was buried, in a little cemetery in West Philadelphia attached to an old Catholic church. I was never one to think much about the past, or visit cemeteries, but now I've been to that little cemetery quite a few times. I found Rose Sullivan Morley's gravestone, and now when I visit I always put a bouquet of flowers by it, and say a prayer or two.

I know I'm connected to her, and everyone who went before.

THE END

THE END OF BOOK SIX

This is the sixth of seven books in the *Rose Of Skibbereen* series. There's one more book in the series after this one. It's called *Mary's Secret,* and it's about Mary Driscoll, a beloved character from Book One. I recommend it if you'd like to revisit the world of the first *Rose Of Skibbereen* book. Look for *Mary's Secret* and the other *Rose of Skibbereen* books on Amazon at:

amazon.com/author/johnmcdonnell.

A word from John McDonnell:

I have been a writer all my life, but after many years of doing other types of writing I'm finally returning to my first love, which is fiction. I write in the horror, sci-fi, romance, humor and fantasy genres, and I have published 24 books on Amazon. I also write plays, and I have a YouTube channel where I post some of them. I live near Philadelphia, Pennsylvania with my wife and four children, and I am a happy man.

My books on Amazon: amazon.com/author/johnmcdonnell.

My YouTube channel:
https://www.youtube.com/user/McDonnellWrite/videos?vie w_as=subscriber

Look me up on Facebook at:
https://www.facebook.com/JohnMcDonnellsWriting/.

Did you like this book? Did you enjoy the characters? Do you have any advice you'd like to give me? I love getting feedback on my books. Send me an email at mcdonnellwrite@gmail.com.

Find all the "Rose Of Skibbereen" books here:

amazon.com/author/johnmcdonnell.

CPSIA information can be obtained
at www.ICGtesting.com
Printed in the USA
LVHW041750190723
752927LV00025B/285